Ways
of
Living

Praise for Ways of Living

'A bold blast of London women weaving their way through the world in their own unique style. Gemma's captivating, perfect-pitch writing makes this a joy to delve into and get lost in different ways of living.'
– Sabrina Mahfouz

'Relationships are at the core of this collection: women's often painful friendships with each other but also with a city that they experience intimately. The characters' deep connections are beautifully written with unexpected, and often gently violent, twists.'
– Alison Winch, author of *Darling, It's Me*

'A sharp, witty collection filled with unforgettable women attempting to navigate both their internal landscapes and the urban spaces they inhabit. I was gripped, delighted, and endlessly surprised.'
– Sarah Butler, author of *Jack & Bet*

'Seltzer is deft when it comes to the permeable boundaries between love and hate, worship and rage, friendship and something darker. This insightful collection shows us that what we feel is not always as straightforward as we might like to believe.'
– Rowan Hisayo Buchanan, author of *Starling Days*

'These are sharp, wry, playful stories of split and secret selves, alter egos, doppelgängers – of escape routes from the very contemporary and existential crises their women find themselves in. I enjoyed them hugely.'
– Lucy Caldwell, author of *Intimacies*

Ways
of
Living

Gemma
Seltzer

Influx Press
London

Published by Influx Press
The Greenhouse
49 Green Lanes, London, N16 9BU
www.influxpress.com / @InfluxPress
All rights reserved.
© Gemma Seltzer, 2021

First edition 2021. Printed and bound in the UK by TJ Books.

Paperback ISBN: 9781910312759
Ebook ISBN: 97819103125766

Editor: Gary Budden
Proofreader: Dan Coxon
Cover design: Luke Bird
Interior design: Vince Haig

Contents

Too Close and
Not Close Enough

Sadie wants the bagel with salt beef and plenty of mustard. She wants it hot, but not so hot she'll burn her mouth. She says she wants the bagel sliced in half, do they do it sliced? Can she have pickles, and also can she have two shakes of pepper?

'Two shakes?' asks the woman behind Beigel Bake's counter. Her hand hovers near the pile of fresh bagels. Each is open and plump, layered with tongues of meat. 'I've worked here for fifteen years,' she says, 'and no one ever said exactly *two* shakes.'

Sadie whoops and clasps her hands together as though she's won a prize. Her necklace catches Brick Lane's sunlight shining through the glass doors. People along the queue comment and smile. Two men in high vis jackets call to her.

'What can I say?' she replies, scrunching her hair on one side. 'I know what I want.'

I'm sixth in line and, like everyone else, like everyone always did, I'm watching her. We haven't seen each other since school.

I'd arrived in the middle of term, moving from my parents' house in Luton to my cousin's place on the edge of London. I was small, shy and played the violin. Unexpectedly and swiftly, lots of girls singled me out as their friend. Many wanted to be in plays or on television. I would watch them arrange their hair by their lockers and listen to their complaints about others. When I first saw Sadie, I thought she was beautiful. She noticed I was from out of town. 'I like new things,' she said, linking arms one day. We were fourteen when we started to spend time out of school together.

Sadie liked to create alternative versions of me. I remembered one time in particular. We sat in my front garden and she spat into a palette of mascara, the kind they made in the sixties, to mix a black paste with the tiny brush. She drew the wand along my lashes. 'The trick is to work slowly,' she said. 'It builds up with each application.' After blowing on my eyelashes, she said, 'I have five layers on today.' She held up a mirror to my face. 'Do you like it?' I nodded, turning my head from side to side. 'You look amazing. You look like a different person.'

The woman says, 'Two shakes.' Opening the bagel, she adds the pepper and the pickles, then spreads mustard on top.

Sadie steps backwards from the counter, digging around in her purse. Her eyelids are pastel-coloured with a meticulous dark arch of eyeshadow in the socket crease. She has radiant red lips. We're both in our late thirties, and she's tremendous with it.

'Hey,' I call over as casually as I can. 'Sadie?'

Sadie snaps her purse closed and looks at me. She says nothing.

'Your hair looks great,' I say. I didn't think I'd see her again but if I ever imagined the moment, this was always my first line.

'You really think so?' She tucks a strand behind her

Gemma Seltzer

ear. 'Juliet,' she says. 'Been such a long time since I thought of you.'

I was dedicated to Sadie. I kept notebooks of everything she liked (pink lipstick, peonies, greyhounds) and what she didn't (rabbits, strong tea, eyebrow piercings). On weekends, it was the two of us. We played her parents' vinyl in her bedroom, listening to every song. Or, we'd watch videos. Her favourite was *The Graduate*. It wasn't only the mascara: we loved everything from the sixties. I'd read Nell Dunn's *Poor Cow* and made us watch the film version again and again. I wanted to be like the main character Joy, who pushed her pram across London pavements with her backcombed hair and a sad, but hopeful, internal monologue. 'All any woman wants is a man and a baby,' says Joy in the film.

Sadie's eyes drift across my body. She is searching for something to say. 'You know, I like your top,' she says. 'Classic styling.'

My shirt has a toothpaste stain on it, which I'd tried to wipe away with a fraying tissue. An embroidered design over the pocket may have once been a fruit basket. I say, 'Well, that's a lie and we both know it.'

Sadie bursts into laughter. 'Yeah, it's horrid. Where the hell did you get it from?'

I smile and we hug, and she tells me all the things she has done and all the people she still knows from school. No mention of a family. She is head of marketing for an independent clothes label and teaches young fashion designers as part of a community entrepreneurship scheme.

There is pride in her voice when she speaks.

'Sounds amazing,' I say. I watch her talk, her small mouth stretching in all directions. It's fair to say I loved Sadie and she loved me. It's equally true that I spent a large proportion of my teenage years hating her, while simultaneously wanting to be her. After twenty years, nothing has changed.

'What about you?' asks Sadie, shifting her bag on her shoulder. 'What do you do?'

As I'm about to answer, the woman behind the counter waves for my attention. 'Planning on ordering anytime soon?'

'Hi!' I say to her, glad for the interruption. 'How are you?' I ask but she's already looking down the queue. I smile brightly. 'I'd love a peanut butter on poppy seed.'

The woman grimaces and holds out her hand for my money. She's already raising her chin for the next person's order when I thank her.

Sadie and I agree to stay a while and catch up. We take our bagels to the high ledge in the shop. She leans back, I stand by her side. Mirror tiles screwed to the wall hold the reflection of her hair. The shop is busy with a constant flow of people queueing for bagels. I tell her about the work I do and where I live.

'You know, I remember at your cousin's house the garage always smelled of sweat,' she says. 'Why was that?'

I shrug. 'Such a weird thing to remember.'

She bites her bagel. She bites again. Mustard oozes from the sides. 'So good.'

We're talking about the teachers we remember when the men in the high vis jackets appear next to us and want to know if we're enjoying the bagels. Both have shaved heads and wedding rings. There's a high volume of winking.

Gemma Seltzer

They're staring at Sadie and I stare at them. They'd travel across London for these bagels, they say. Best in the world. Sadie asks them how old they are.

'I'm in the neighbourhood of fifty,' one says.

'You should move to a different part of town,' grins the other.

They all laugh and chat together while I pull off bagel pieces and chew them with my mouth open. One of Sadie's arms now tucks under her chest, the other holds the bagel aloft. She isn't eating it anymore and she probably won't eat it now.

'My cousin exercised in there, that's why,' I say, cutting into the conversation. 'Weights and press-ups, that kind of thing.'

The three of them stop talking. Sadie looks at me as if remembering I'm there. She is so close I can smell her: fresh bedsheets and vanilla.

Sadie nods. 'Makes sense.'

One of the men opens his mouth to speak, but I jump in again. 'I changed my name. I'm not Juliet anymore.'

She raises an eyebrow to her new friends. 'Really?'

I squeeze the remains of my bagel in its paper. 'It's actually...' I find I can't say the words.

Sadie smiles but her tone is sharp. 'You may as well tell us now.'

Our younger selves are like dogs on leads, straining to reach each other, barking into each other's faces. We're holding on tight, but I'm about to set mine free.

'Okay, fine.' I raise my voice. 'It's Sadie.'

She stops grinning.

'Are you serious?' says Sadie.

A man in a flat cap at the counter is ordering three dozen

bagels. It's his twin sons' birthday, he tells everyone. He's excited. The bagels will be piled high like a cake.

'Sadie,' I say, louder than I planned but there it is, out in the world.

'Nice name,' says one of the men.

'I think so. I've had it for a few years now. There was quite a bit of paperwork to do, but once it's done, it's done.'

Sadie puts her sandwich on the ledge, gently, as if it is precious. To the men, she says, 'Nice name? Of course it is. It's mine. She's changed her name to my name.'

'What?' say the men, now uncertain of their position in the conversation. They only wanted a post-bagel flirt.

'Yeah, I'm Sadie now,' I say.

We went to a music festival. The August sun was hot, the sky huge and blue. A group of us met in the morning at the bus stop. There was no shelter. Where we lived was beyond the end of a tube line, barely London. The boys had baggy clothes and kicked at the kerb. The girls were all limbs in shorts and cotton vest tops. We missed the first bus, sticky in the sunshine while waiting for Sadie. Cars and vans rumbled along the road. A breeze blew and, glad for it, I closed my eyes. When I opened them again, Sadie was walking towards us, waving and harassed. She wore white-framed sunglasses and a golden camisole with lace tickling the neck and hem. Beneath it, a cerise push-up bra.

'Sorry, sorry.' Sadie mentioned delays on the Northern line and an argument with her sister.

One of the boys joked she was wearing her underwear, and had she forgotten to get dressed? Her hair trailed down her back. I thought she looked phenomenal and I decided to grow mine long, too.

'You look so pretty.' I hugged her close as my way of saying she should ignore them and, also, hello.

In the dance tent, we moved to Sneaker Pimps. Arms raised above, heads scooping the air. Her dress clung to her skin as if damp. I had an eye on her throughout; we all did. It was strange to see her in a large crowd. Everyone else, our friends and the strangers, looked grey as rooftops by comparison.

We walked to find food and she pulled at her bra a great deal, yanking the straps and jiggling the underwire. The chorus from a song we knew rose from one of the stages. Fried onion smells filled the air. By a group of men, she dabbed glitter along my cheeks. She made me roll my vest top under itself to make a crop top. We ran around together, shrieking under a fountain of water, sharing a pack of chips, my stomach bare and daring. On the way back to the others, she crouched down to adjust her trainer. Her loose dress fell forward.

'Sadie, what are you doing?' I whispered. 'You're showing everyone everything. You look so dumb.' The weather felt hot and prickly on my neck.

She stood upright and her eyes were wet. 'I thought you said I looked pretty?'

Sadie has my arm and is leading me out of the shop. It's late afternoon, the red sun is dropping in the sky. 'Is that a Pret a Manger? It used to be so rough around here.' She stares ahead as we walk while, all along the crowded street, people wander and pause by shop windows. By the Truman

Brewery, a man sits in a doorway, crutches leaning against the nearby wall. His hands are cupped and held upwards, his head facing the paving stones.

'Poor guy,' says Sadie.

She releases me but stays close. While she's digging in her bag, I look around. Several groups are having tours and taking photos of themselves against graffiti backgrounds.

'Here you go,' Sadie says to the man and tucks a note between his fingers. He doesn't look up. 'Okay,' she says to him, or to herself. 'Okay. It's fine. It's fine.'

I know this part of London well, and point towards a quieter street where there's a nice bookshop and a few cafes.

As we walk, Sadie speaks quietly. 'You can't do this, Juliet. I just don't...' Her hands are in fists. 'How is it possible to take someone else's name?' She wants to call the police, she says it is identity theft. 'Of all the names in the world, why would you pick mine?'

'First of all,' I say, 'a name is only a name. It doesn't have to mean anything.' I have reasoned this in my mind for many years. 'Secondly, I liked the name, okay? It's actually a compliment. Third of all—'

Sadie shakes her head. 'That's not a thing.'

We arrive at the bookshop. There are fairy lights and inside several armchairs with people leafing through magazines and novels. If I was alone, I'd go inside and lose myself for an hour or so.

I say, 'Well, thirdly, then, there's always more than one John Smith. If it's a good name, a lot of people want it.'

'Call yourself John Smith then.'

Several insistent car sirens sound close to us. We stand together in silence, looking around us until the commotion dies away.

Weekends we often spent at Camden Market. I had a dark bob and a thick fringe. We held hands and wandered into dusty shops playing Joan Baez records. We liked the cavernous emporiums with psychedelic murals and rails filled with dresses, scarves and creased leather shoes.

Once, painting our nails by the canal, she put her head on my shoulder and said I was her best friend. We flapped our wrists to dry the varnish and admired the colours. She said she liked my red nails and I quickly offered her the little jar I'd bought. She took it, delighted. I'd have pulled out each of my fingernails and given them to her if she said she wanted them, and she knew that. We were happy.

In my bedroom later that day, I listened to Portishead while a lava lamp formed and reformed waxy bubbles. Sadie had given me one of her shopping bags and now, in the mirror, I was admiring my reflection. 'Take a photo,' she'd said as we waved goodbye. The sunglasses looked good, as did her lipstick around my mouth. I dropped her silk nightie over my head and watched it spill down my body, before settling, silent. It was the closest I'd ever felt to her.

Every cafe is too busy. The one we end up in has a glass ceiling pouring exceptionally hot sunlight into the seating area and making the wooden surfaces glow. There's a spare table in a corner which I suggest, but even here we have to squint in the vivid light. A man with a big beard takes our order. When he asks for a name, we answer at the same time: 'Sadie.'

Sadie slams her hand on the table causing the menu to jump. '*She* is not Sadie. I'm Sadie!'

'We've been over this,' I say, giving the man a conspiratorial roll of my eyes, and I pull out my driver's licence. He nods, looking at Sadie. On the shiny pink surface there's a Union Jack, my looping signature and, typed in capitals, my name.

'Give me that.' Sadie snatches the card from my hand. 'I'll need this when I speak to the lawyer. I can get a lawyer, you know.'

Then she starts talking about her personal freedom. Her friend of a friend who worked at a law firm. A story about her mother told in a quick, defensive tone. Her thoughts are circling above us.

A different man calls out our name because our coffees are ready. We both wave. She barely pauses when he brings them over. I listen to Sadie, although not to every word. It's like washing up while the radio is on in the background. The makeup on her face is pristine, except for a smudge on one eyelid. I think: I'm with Sadie. After all these years. Sadie.

I open my mouth to speak. The fact she is here, thinking aloud in the cafe, makes me wonder if she's as angry as she says. Perhaps she likes the attention.

'I haven't finished,' she says, recognising my attempt to interrupt.

'Go on,' I say.

She twists her hair into a loose bun, and I take a sip of my coffee.

We leaned over a bridge in the park, throwing sticks into

Gemma Seltzer

gloomy water and passing around a vodka bottle. Other girls were there, but Sadie and I stood apart. Being alone with Sadie was always a relief. As if we were camping in a zipped-up tent, hidden inside against the pummelling rain. The river flowed swiftly, but the edges were thick with algae and chocolate wrappers. 'Guess what? Tonight, I'm going to beat my record.' As time went on, Sadie changed. Her mission now when we went out was to meet older men. She'd let them kiss her in exchange for a drink. 'Do you dare me to go for ten?' I laughed, but felt my blood drop into my feet. 'Tell me how to wear my hair,' she said, gathering the strands on top of her head before letting it fall over her shoulders. I said, 'Down, I think.' She wrinkled her nose. 'No, it's better up.'

At the club later, our gang of girls huddled together by the stage and drank alcopops. We swayed to the music, laughing too loud and knocking against each other. Sadie leaned towards me and said, 'I'll be back in a minute.' I chatted with the others, publicly admiring everyone's clothes while secretly feeling they should've chosen another top or another skirt. The crowd cheered as the drummer leaped on stage, then the guitarist and singer appeared. I clapped my bottle against my hand. As the band started playing, I looked around and saw Sadie kissing a skinny guy whose hands hung by his sides. One of our friends was at the bar. I spotted Darius, a boy from the year above who played violin too, who saluted in my direction. I smiled, alarmed but pleased.

The smoke machine puffed out by our feet. I craned my neck and saw Sadie with a shorter man with long sideburns. I turned away, listening to the music and clapping at the end of each song. Near the middle of the set, I glanced around and saw Sadie on the lap of a man with a shaved head.

For the final song, everyone at the front threw their bodies together. A voice called out, 'Mosh pit!' My friends and I threw ourselves into the mass of people, bouncing between the bass from the speakers. Sweaty flesh touched damp skin squashed against wet hair. I wondered where Darius was and then I saw his head pop up nearby. He waved at me again. A woman dived off the stage and we both held her above our heads, passing her body along from person to person. As the final chords played and the cheers died down, I heard a scream and saw across the room Sadie bent double, vomiting on the floor.

'Sadie!' I was pushing figures out of my way, saying, 'Let me through.' People were not moving quick enough. I kicked at someone's heel and elbowed someone else. Everywhere was noise. Then I was by Sadie's side with my arm around her and using my sleeve to wipe drool from her mouth. 'I'm sorry, I'm really sorry,' she was saying. We stumbled to the toilets which smelled of blackcurrant and vinegar. In a cubicle, I helped her kneel over the bowl and I held back her hair as she was sick. 'You're okay.' I saw on her arm there were bruises. I was shaken and the emotion rising in me was physical. 'Sadie, what are these?' I said. She lifted her head. 'Guy from earlier. The usual.' I pressed damp tissues to her forehead and stroked her head, while she turned to the toilet bowl and retched. One of our friends passed her a pint of water to sip. Sadie was hiccupping and crying.

Outside, I flagged a taxi and we drove back to her house with the back windows open. I didn't see Darius to say goodbye. People drifted out of bars and onto the streets, shouting at each other and stumbling into lampposts. I watched a man smash his glass at another man's feet.

'You'll pay if she throws up on the upholstery,' said the driver, looking at us in the rear-view mirror.

'I won't,' Sadie said, and then vomited down her clothes. I took off my cardigan and dabbed it on her to absorb the mess.

'The smell is worse than the actual sick,' I said to the taxi driver, as if that would help.

We stopped at a cashpoint so I could pay for the journey. It was money from my savings account, but I didn't mind.

As we turned into her street, Sadie said, 'You do it with me next time.'

'What?'

'You just say, "I like you." That's all you say. The guys do the rest.'

'Are you serious?'

'I'll do your hair and your makeup. What do you reckon?'

'Sadie, I'm not you.' What I meant was I wasn't beautiful. I wasn't confident. It was her attention I craved, not theirs. It was a friend I wanted, not some guy.

At Sadie's house I helped her get to bed. I lay down and slept on the air mattress.

Things changed after that. I started spending time with other girls. I didn't answer Sadie's calls. She wrote me letters. I annotated them and sent them back in response. I wasn't kind, I know that. School continued inevitably. Once, we literally bumped into each other entering the door for year assembly and while we locked eyes, neither of us spoke. Sadie and I ended our friendship without a goodbye and without a conclusion.

'Look,' Sadie says. 'What I don't understand is what was wrong with the name "Juliet"? We could call you Jules.'

I rub the toothpaste on my shirt, licking my finger and wiping it over the stain.

She says, 'You know, you were the kind of person people liked. You could have anyone as your friend. People liked you, do you understand that?' Her gaze holds me in place.

'Okay, but the feelings weren't mutual.' I push away my coffee cup and start listing on my fingers. I begin with Bianca, who I sat next to in Chemistry.

Bianca showed me a list titled 'best mates' and I was at the top. When she described me to another friend as a fellow outcast, she felt it was an honourable title. It was for the shy and awkward. The boring and rejected. Bianca was able to feel understood with me by her side.

Sharon said that although I didn't often speak at school, she liked that I smiled a lot.

Olivia said I put up with a lot from her. She was referring to her constant need for reassurance. At the end of our long conversations, she always said, 'Cheers big ears.' I sometimes wondered if she knew my real name.

Kiren ran her eyes over every person's clothes, hair and words. When we were alone, she'd repeat everything she'd seen. 'Natalie had hiccups, but was mortified. You know she insisted that we sing "Beetlebum"? It was to hide her gulps.' Or, 'Vicky had a bogey on her finger for a full five minutes. She couldn't work out what to do with it. She eventually wiped it under her hairline at the back.' Both Kiren and I knew anyone who stepped away from the group risked becoming the subject of discussion, so we often remained anxiously with our legs crossed. I was included in her scrutiny. 'That story you told about getting a tan on Saturday and it fading by Monday? Everyone knew you were lying.'

Sonia and I met at a Jewish summer camp in Wales. She said she'll never forget the night we talked about our lives on the hotel balcony. We were both grateful to finally find someone who was interested in what the other had to say.

Yasmin's eyes would glaze over when I spoke of anything other than lessons and homework. She colour-coded her school timetable. She set her alarm for dawn to read her notes from the day before. She loved the smell of a mock exam paper. When we practised French together, she'd give me directions to her imaginary Paris apartment near Shakespeare and Company. It had shutters, a constant supply of fresh coffee and bean bags instead of chairs.

No one liked Brenda, but she had an older brother in a band.

Deborah dyed her hair blue-black and wore Marilyn Manson sweatshirts. We studied for our Bat Mitzvah ceremony together. My parents would be there, and I wanted to do well. Our teacher Mrs Woolf told us women must focus all their energy on bringing up children with tradition, so we learned about keeping kosher at home and how to knead, twist and bake challah. A few weeks before the event, Mrs Woolf placed a finger flat on my shoulder and ran it down my arm. She asked me to stop her when she'd reached the sleeve length of the jacket I'd wear. 'When!' I called, when she reached my wrist bone, proud of my feminine modesty, then. Deborah packed up her folders at that point. 'I'm done here,' she said.

It isn't hard to remember these girls from my teenage years. They appear standing side by side in my imagination, looking at me, expectant. Sadie wasn't perfect but I knew I could add these other friends together and Sadie would outweigh them all.

The heat from the cafe skylight is still strong, but we're used to it now. I'm not sure when Sadie stopped talking. Her eyes flick back and forth.

I tip my coffee cup towards me now, considering the remains. I realise what I want to say. 'The name thing. I guess it's an apology.'

'An apology?' says Sadie, leaning forward.

'A messy one, but yes: I'm sorry.'

Gemma Seltzer

Other Esther

We meet Esther for the first time waking up in a Travelodge bathtub wearing her swimsuit. The water is lukewarm, and the bubbles have dissolved. She's lying with her head against the edge and her throat's dry from too much gin but when she clutches for her plastic cup, it's empty and slips to the floor. Rubbing her eyes brings a sore, lonely kind of pain. The time is exactly two a.m., although Esther doesn't know that. She shakes her ankles.

Something taps her leg. It's rough and sodden. Her eyes flash open. She sees Other Esther floating face down.

'Oh god.' Esther leaps up. Her dad is going to kill her. 'Oh god.'

The next part happens quickly, pay attention: Esther grabs Other Esther, bringing her up with a torrent of water. The ceiling fan screams. Esther leaps out of the bath, snatches for a towel and wraps it around them both.

'What happened?' Esther asks, laying Other Esther on the bathmat. Shaking her, she shouts, 'Can you hear me?'

Esther sees water leak from Other Esther's jaw. She rolls her sideways and bends her elbows and knees into something like the recovery position. The hair is a matted mess. Driving a comb through it would be impossible; Esther can imagine the fury in Other Esther's voice if she even tried.

Raphael has the bath sponge above Esther. 'Mr Sponge needs a wee!' he says, squeezing water onto her hair.

Esther shrieks and splashes in the bathtub, her toys bobbing on the surface. Other Esther screams. She's sitting on a chair in the far corner because she disagrees with too much steam.

'Pipe on down!' says Raphael over his shoulder to Other Esther.

She replies, 'Just you wait 'til I'm bigger than you!'

Light streams through a stained-glass window painting their faces and bodies light blue and red. Raphael dips the sponge in and threatens another dribble, but then drops it in the water. Esther pats at the bubbles. 'They are sparkling,' she says.

'They are, darling.' Raphael cups her chin and smiles. He lifts Esther and whirls her around several times. When she's on the bathmat, he instructs her to count her years.

One. Esther shakes the drips from her hair. Two. She wiggles her body. Three. She swivels around. Four! She jumps up. Five! In his arms, he holds out a towel and she leaps into its soft goodness.

'Keep going!' Raphael spins her around and around until she loses any sense of where she stops and where the towel begins. 'And the other way!' Esther is stumbling in circles, guided by hands and towel.

'Go, go!' says Other Esther.

Esther turns faster and faster, until finally she drops. Raphael brings her to his lap, feeling her heart beating. He squeezes her tightly and kisses her head. She's on the verge of tears, unsure about the dizziness now.

'Where's Other Esther?' she asks in a small voice.

Gemma Seltzer

Raphael sets down Esther and reaches towards the chair for Other Esther. He notices her cheeks are damp and seem flushed. They all sit quietly together, and Esther takes Other Esther's hand to hold in her own. It curves like a lemon.

Three bodies on a bathmat, in a corner of the city, on the best evening ever.

The train jerks away from London Bridge station. Other Esther is in a wicker carrycot on the seat next to Esther. She's tucked under several blankets that reach her nose. Esther keeps adjusting the pillows and fiddling with the straps.

'Leave me alone, I'm sleeping,' says Other Esther.

Without Raphael, the voice isn't right. He had years of practice, of course. Opposite sits a man with a cap and headphones, his eyes closed. Esther sits back and looks at her phone. Eighteen missed calls from her dad and loads of WhatsApp messages including family photos. She takes in the view from the window. Waiting on the train platform at Blackfriars, she notices a number of women standing alone, rummaging in a bag, involved in a book or staring at the tracks. She reaches under the blanket to touch Other Esther's bare leg and wishes she could see the sky.

At King's Cross, teenagers burst into the train carriage. Their teacher has a whistle that he blows. 'Find a seat, find a seat!' he calls, but they congregate near the doorway and along the aisles. Esther's heart pumps fast. We understand her thinking. None of this would make sense to anyone else. *No, it's not a baby in here. No.* So, it's not a surprise that she's soon stepping onto the platform, aiming towards the exit with the carrycot held to her chest.

Outside the station, there's a row of shops then the road bends and leads to a long brown and concrete hotel building with four arches leading to a car park. It has identical flat windows like tired eyes. Esther sympathises.

'Just for you, is it?' says the woman behind the Travelodge counter. The price for a single is low because these rooms are in the older part of the building. 'Or would you prefer something with a bit more space?'

Esther shakes her head and signs the forms. The lift delivers them to the third floor. As soon as they arrive, she unwraps Other Esther. 'You're not hurt?' she asks.

'I'm fine, no thanks to you,' Other Esther says.

One of her pigtails is crooked and there are flecks of white on her dress. The two of them lie there, thinking their own thoughts. Esther follows the trail of clouds outside. It was clever of Esther to take the train but remain in London. Her dad probably thinks they've travelled down to the sea or up to Scotland. By now, he'll probably have noticed his cash from the cabinet is gone. The bank might have filled him in on the rest of the story.

After a while, Esther says, 'How about we freshen you up? I could do your hair, maybe?' She leans over to take a handful of Wet Ones from her bag. 'We'll rest here for a bit.'

'Finally, a good idea from you.' Other Esther sounds like a stranger.

'I think we're both tired, aren't we?' Esther says and she feels older, like a parent.

Other Esther hums as her face is stroked with the wipe, and then her hair is brushed and plaited.

Gemma Seltzer

'Do you love me?' Esther asks.

There is no reply.

Raphael loosens the box lid. He sees a layer of brown paper, then bubble wrap around a swatch of velvet. What would Marianne have kept in here? Could be shoes, or wellies. Family heirloom? Her dad is in the house with everyone else downstairs, so he could ask, but the man barely moved that morning at the funeral. Only glared at the mound of soil by the grave.

Lifting the fabric, Raphael sees it's a doll. A blond, pig-tailed, plastic-faced doll. No, a dummy. A ventriloquist's figure with a painted red mouth. He lets out a sigh and sits with his back against the wall.

'Well,' he says, taking the doll in his arms. She smells of shoe polish and sand. Her long-lashed eyes stare into his. He says, 'Hello there. What will I do with you?'

In the classroom, Raphael gathers people with hand movements and encouragement, as if sweeping together autumn leaves. Everyone stands in a circle and one by one they step forward to present themselves and their puppet.

Marigold is first and she says, 'This is my friend, Nancy.' She's a blond shepherdess who has lost her sheep. The figure hangs over her arm, barely alive.

'Hello everyone!' says Nancy.

Marigold grimaces as if she wishes she were anywhere but the class. 'Was that okay?'

They all say friendly things. A man with a sock puppet giggles. Other Esther lowers her chin to nod. Raphael scans the room and notes a muppet with fuzzy blue hair. Generic factory-made import, no doubt. They hear from a guy with a shaggy dog called Wayne who lives in his satchel. Raphael is more impressed. Performing with a puppet peering from a bag is a classic move.

He's covering a session on puppetry for this children's entertainment course last minute as the original teacher fell ill that morning. Raphael has barely thought about what he'll teach but he's not worried as he's run similar workshops. Storytelling, engaging audiences and ending with a flourish. Those are his core principles, so that's how he'll structure the session. He is a professional. It's not like he could turn down work at the moment, and the pay is pretty decent.

'I'm Raphael,' he says when it's his turn to present himself. 'A ventriloquist.' Was that a murmur of appreciation from the group? There's more he wants to say, let's listen. 'Puppetry, with fluffy figures of differing sizes, is the simpler art. It mesmerises children. It's full of movement, such as flying, dancing, singing, to keep audiences entertained. At the other end of the scale is ventriloquism. The ability to speak fluidly without the mouth moving is a fine one. Raising and lowering the voice, changing its speed and direction, takes years of practice.'

'And, of course, the right partner!' says Other Esther.

It's a pristine voice, which gives Raphael extreme satisfaction. The tone, the sound, the *expression*, was exactly as he had hoped.

'Who is this modest creature?' asks a tall man wearing a cravat.

　　　　　　　　　　　　　　　Gemma Seltzer

'I am Other Esther.' She bows.

The man holds a purple hippo which has a garland of flowers around its neck. 'I'm Philip. Meet Hip Hippo. The coolest cat, but of course not a cat.'

Other Esther swings her head in Hip's direction and lifts her hand. 'Would you hold this for me, while we go for a walk?'

'He will certainly not,' Raphael says, capturing her fingers and pressing them to her chest. 'I'd like us to agree some ground rules.' The group discusses this and decides a few together including listening respectfully and being open to learning.

Meanwhile, Other Esther waves at Hip again, and Raphael moves to grab her hand but keeps missing.

'Let's focus,' he says. 'Together we will explore all kinds of territory. You'll agree to be characters you despise. You'll invent scenarios you'd hate.' Raphael speaks about flow and creativity, about losing yourself in a story.

Towards the end of his talk, Other Esther presses her face into his shoulder. Every so often she glances at Hip. 'Please take my hand.'

Philip looks to his puppet. 'You have an admirer, no?'

'You're such a square, man,' says Hip, shaking his head. 'Cramping my style.'

'I don't need you.' Philip sounds angry. 'I can be funny without a puppet!'

Hip says, 'You aren't funny with a puppet.'

Everyone laughs. Other Esther blows kisses towards Hip. In this top floor classroom with exposed brick walls and the smell of dust hanging heavy in the air, Raphael has a feeling that everything is as it should be.

In the pub, men with stubble and small eyes laugh when Esther orders two bottles of Budweiser and curry meals. It is the first offer listed on the menu. With all the cash she has and her driving licence, she can buy everything behind the bar, so she's surprised her hand is shaking as she passes the ten-pound note.

'Girls' night out,' she says in her most confident voice, tipping her head towards Other Esther in her carrycot.

As they wait for their food at a table, Esther smiles at everyone who passes as though this is all a joke. She's ploughing through her phone, looking at maps and Twitter, and reading messages from her dad. He'll know she's online. Other Esther sits in her case, head flopping to one side. They're hiding in full sight, really. It's not like they planned this. But now, here they are, sitting in a pub on Euston Road, living in a Travelodge. It could be worse.

'Couldn't it?' she asks Other Esther.

'What? Am I a mind reader?'

The waitress appears with their food and abandons the two plates without a word. The white rice is piled in a mound and the soil-coloured curry sauce has sprigs of fresh coriander.

Alcohol loosens Esther's tongue. She finishes her drink and takes the second bottle. They chat and laugh about the old days. If Esther is not actually relaxed, she pretends to be. Her mood lifts. Towards the end of the night, it's Other Esther who tugs on Esther's sleeve and says it's time to go.

Gemma Seltzer

Raphael is learning substitutions. He's in the kitchen facing a long mirror propped against the table. The figure is on his knee and he's practising making sounds *like* the letters he wants to say. For some consonants, you gently rest the lower lip on the top set of teeth. For others, you push your tongue against the upper gums. 'Knock knock, etc, etc,' he says. 'Aladdin who?'

He answers himself in a high voice. '"Aladdin the station. Thell on the wail track." Fell on the rail track?' He's getting better. Raphael rests his chin on the figure's head for a moment. She has been repaired and cleaned. For the plastic and wooden parts, he mixed white vinegar and water in a spray bottle and gave her a scrub. She has a new wig with plaits on each side. The doll's face was wiped with a damp cloth and then she was doused in orange flower water.

'What happened to Aladdin?'

Raphael yawns to relax his vocal folds. The doll squeaks her lines. He tries again, this time lower and quieter. The trick is to keep talking to the doll, chatting back and forth, until you find a voice which fits. He looks at her face and pulls the same expression. He echoes hers in his. Full lips. Bottom set of teeth on show. Eyes wide.

'"Fell on the rail tracks,"' he says, drawing out each word. Might be it. Raphael lifts her hand and presses it into the air for emphasis. It's tiring, though, to switch between your voice and the figure's voice, but Raphael keeps going until he has it right. When he sneezes, she has something to say.

'"Goodness!"'

That's a surprise and makes him laugh. He strokes her plaits. The light outside is milky. He's calm for a while. That bank loan may come through, he thinks, hopeful as ever. The clock flicks over to four o'clock. He should be washing up. The sink is piled with pans and plates. He should have done some ironing. There's dinner to make, as well. He has been here since two.

'"Can I haf a hug?"' The figure reaches out her arms. '"He died."'

'I'm very sorry. There, there.' Squeezing the body, Raphael holds her close and she snuggles upwards. It is time to wake Esther, but he will wait a few minutes yet.

Des has a cricket bat called Batty who is incredibly fidgety and so is thumped repeatedly on Des' open palm. Batty has two eyes and a mouth drawn with coloured pens. It's not the most sophisticated of puppets, but for the first workshop of the course, Raphael will let it go. They are all working together on an exercise called 'continuous exchanges'.

Raphael uses the rod attached to Other Esther's forearm and has her gesture towards Batty. 'Are you okay down there?' she says to the bat.

'Yeah,' says Des.

'Try to let Batty answer,' says Raphael.

Other Esther nods and says, 'I've got a lot of knock knock jokes in my head. It's getting noisy and my knuckles hurt from pounding the doors so hard.'

'What's she on about?' asks Des, whacking Batty down again.

'I'm finding this a tad distracting,' says Raphael. 'Try going back and forth with her. Keep it moving.'

Batty rises again, his expressionless face close to Raphael's own.

'Try again, ask Other Esther anything.'

'Why are you called Other Esther?'

'Make Batty say it.'

Des lifts his voice into the back of his throat. It's a sound like someone suppressing a cough but at least he's found a different tone for his puppet. '"Why are you called Other Esther?"'

'Good, good,' says Raphael. 'I think you're really onto something now.'

'I am,' says Batty, pausing on Des' palm.

'You are,' Raphael raises his hand for a high five, which they manage by turning to the side. 'Okay, let me tell you the story about her name, then.'

Bad weather in the night wakes Esther. The window frames rattle from the pounding rain. She's four years old and it's been a year since her mother died. He can't see too much of a difference, but she is quiet. Their friends say so, too. She won't call out if she's upset. So, Raphael doesn't hear her leave her bed and climb down the stairs. He doesn't expect her body in the kitchen doorway, looking at him there at the table with the figure on his knee.

'Who's she?' whispers Esther.

Raphael has to think quickly. There is a rumble of thunder outside, and Esther's eyes are huge. 'Darling,' he says, buying himself some time as he puts down the doll and extends his hand for his daughter. She's a good girl, she has her slippers on, so her feet keep warm. He rubs his hand along her arm. 'You're okay, don't be scared.'

'Don't like it,' she says, tears winding their way silently down her face.

She looks so small, Raphael thinks. How can anyone be that small? 'Look, let me introduce you to my new friend, she needs somewhere to stay. She hasn't got anybody who loves her.'

Esther watches. She says, 'Hasn't she got a daddy?'

'No,' says Raphael, gently.

'Or a mummy?'

'No.'

'Where does she live?'

'I don't know.' He turns to the doll. 'Where do you live?'

The figure shakes its head and closes its eyes. The cord for that action is stiff and Raphael will need to fix it. 'Shall we ask her for a joke?'

Esther nods. The rain seems to let up slightly.

'"Knock knock,"' the figure says.

Raphael replies, 'Who's there?'

'"Cows go."'

'Cows go who?'

'"No, silly. Cows go moo!"' The figure falls about laughing, her jaw clacking and her body shaking at the same time. '"Cows go moo!"'

'They go moo!' says Esther.

Raphael slaps his leg, accepting the mockery. 'Daddy is so silly.'

'"Mooooo!"' the figure says. He keeps making the noise, partly because he is not sure he can maintain his ventriloquist voice for too long.

Esther giggles. The tears feel far away, now. 'What's her name?'

His hand is damp, working the rods in the chest cavity. He looks at Esther, who is mesmerised. He's been spending a lot of time with the figure. Staying up late to practise and reading everything he can find on ventriloquism. It's been a good distraction. There are quiet days at the office, and his boss mentioned they might have to reduce his hours. He's been wondering whether there's anything he could do with the doll, performances of some kind. He thinks he'd enjoy it. 'What do you think her name is?'

Her eyes rise to the ceiling. 'I think her name is Esther.'

'Esther?'

'Yes.'

'But that's your name. We can't have two Esthers in the family.'

Esther has an answer ready. 'She can be the other Esther, then.'

It's easier to leave the Travelodge with Other Esther now, as she's comfortable enough on Esther's hip. If someone approaches, Esther says her friend is shy. Once, at the supermarket entrance, Esther hears a siren and starts to worry that she has a disease that makes her heart pummel so often and so hard. She doesn't, of course, but you understand the thinking. Other Esther is in the trolley seat at the front, her legs hanging through the gaps. They pick up fruit in packages, milk cartons and paper plates.

'Get more crisps,' says Other Esther.

'Fine,' Esther replies.

'Get Hobnobs and Haribo. Get some lemons for your gin.' She lists more things as they pass the items in the aisles.

It's not easy to care for a ventriloquist's dummy. They can't keep quiet, and you can't make them. They talk continuously, out loud and in your mind.

In the bakery section, fresh crusty baguettes are piled in a basket marked as half price. Raphael loves this kind of bread, how the soft, powdery smell takes only a moment to work its magic. Esther selects one and takes her phone from her back pocket.

'What shall I say? To him,' she asks, fingers poised above the keypad.

They think through the different ways to tell Raphael they are okay. A man around Esther's age with a dark jacket stops and asks if she is making a film. She has to think quickly. She's getting good at that. It's as though she's acting a part. Esther glances over her shoulder as if for the crew. Lowering her voice, she says it's for a documentary. It'll be on Channel 4. 'Don't tell anyone,' she whispers.

'Cool, cool,' the man says, adjusting his collar so he's smart enough for the screen. 'What's the story?'

Esther tells him it's about obsession.

Esther walks into the classroom and feels rage immediately. Raphael's mouth is rolling around talking at everyone. She stands by the door, watching him laugh hard and show his yellow, lopsided teeth. When he spots her, he waves.

'Hey, Dad. Hey, Other Esther,' she says. 'Having fun?'

Gemma Seltzer

Other Esther doesn't hide her feelings. 'Did the security guard let you in?'

'That's a fine welcome.'

Raphael didn't play favourites when they were young. If he bought one a new bike, the other had one too. He briefly remembers when he taught Other Esther to cycle. Stabilisers on, spent ages strapping her legs to the pedals and fixing her hands to the handlebars. That was the day Esther had the accident, spinning out of control when his back was turned. She crashed into a low brick wall and fell onto the paving stones. 'Darling.' He doesn't direct his comment to either of them. 'You saw my note then? How come you're here?'

'I just wanted to see you,' says Esther.

Raphael's face is in constant motion; his mind processing information and filtering details, then slotting them in place. 'Tonight?'

Other Esther looks at the floor.

'Yes,' says Esther. 'I thought I'd wander over.' She didn't want an evening at home alone and the college is not too far from where they live.

Raphael's nostrils flare, his ears twitch. 'Okay.'

Philip joins them and launches into the conversation. 'Is it your fault he's so good at this, then?' he says, shaking her hand. 'I'm Philip.'

Esther holds his gaze for a moment. It's always like this: there are always other people around her dad. She says, 'He used to be really bad, but I made him write down ideas and start scripting his jokes. Whenever we went somewhere, I'd make him notice and remember what he saw.'

'She did!' says Raphael. 'I remember.'

Other Esther stretches her neck towards Hip, but he seems keen on Esther.

'Yeah,' Esther says. 'He'd bring a notebook and I'd say, good, great. Every moment is an opportunity to be seized, Dad. Don't spend time listening to me drone on about school and my exams. No, you write things you overhear at the next table. Just make it seem as if you're listening to me, so they don't notice, I said.' She feels that strange quick satisfaction people have when they're unkind to someone they love.

'Not quite like that,' says Raphael.

'Like I was someone important, being interviewed. I'd suggest he moved his chair to make sure he could see the other diners. Don't even worry about whether I'm enjoying my food, I'd say.' Esther is smiling as she speaks. 'Hello little man,' she says, stroking the hippo's head. 'Aren't you sweet.'

'I am, I am,' says Hip, nuzzling into her fingers.

Other Esther folds her arms. It will take a while for her to shift this mood.

'Well, he's certainly an impressive man and it sounds like you've been a very attentive daughter,' says Philip.

'She has,' Raphael says.

'I have.' She continues to stroke Hip and he starts to purr.

'What a great class,' says Philip. 'What a great group.'

They all turn away from the conversation to observe the room. The final part of the evening is open for people to explore improvisation skills. One man has a puppet in a headlock. Nancy, for some reason, is face down on the floor while Marigold tiptoes around her body.

Esther says, 'I stopped talking after a while, Phil, so he could fully concentrate on capturing, I don't know, the way the waitress coughed twice.'

Gemma Seltzer

Philip picks dust from Hip's head. 'I should join the others,' he says and drifts away.

'Do you want to do something after the class,' says Raphael in a low voice. 'Get some food.'

Two people start chanting a sea shanty, and Raphael looks over to give a thumbs up. 'There'll be places open.'

'*I'm* having a steak,' says Other Esther.

'Looking forward to that weekend away we have planned, too.'

'Okay,' Esther sighs. 'But I'm pretty tired tonight. Can it just be the two of us?'

'*I'm* part of the family!'

'I feel like I want—'

'Just the three of us!' sings Other Esther, rocking from side to side.

'Shh, a minute,' says Esther. 'Dad, could we—'

'We can make it if we try,' continues Raphael. You'll see Raphael is trying to lighten the mood.

'There's things I want to say and for once I thought it'd be nice to put on smart clothes and mark this moment—'

'This is my moment,' sings Other Esther, doing her stupid giggle

Esther can't handle it anymore and in a quick, sharp motion, she slaps Other Esther's cheek. Raphael feels the impact along his arm. The students stop mid-performance, with puppets held above their heads. 'I'm sorry,' says Esther, staring at her fingers and shaking her head. 'God. I don't know what's got into me.' She looks up at Other Esther. 'I'm so sorry.'

'It's that time again!' Esther calls from the bathroom.

'Am I supposed to be excited?' Other Esther replies.

Esther laughs. 'Such a delight, aren't you?'

They have habits now. Esther runs a bath and pours in Radox bubbles. She lowers herself into the water. The first night she bathed without clothes in here and the surge of loneliness hit her within seconds. The next night, she decided to slip on her swimsuit and prop Other Esther beside the taps. It was better and now this is the routine. Esther has also started bringing a drink. Most evenings, they talk about their childhood. When they would make paper airplanes and aim them towards the clouds. When they'd take turns on the garden swing. When they wore matching clothes.

'Those horses you had in the bath? What were they called?' asks Other Esther.

Esther lets her talk for a while. Her voice is a warm jacket. Along with the hot water, she lets herself be covered by it. 'Sea ponies!'

'Oh yes, Esther! Yes!'

Look, Esther knows she's a doll. Don't think she doesn't.

One great and successful evening was too much for Raphael to hope for. Laying Other Esther on the ground by his feet, he notices a small crack along her cheek. He takes Esther's hand in his, examining for damage. She doesn't jerk away. 'Darling,' he says.

Raphael directs Esther to a chair and has her sit. He says to the group they should think about how anger plays a role in their performances. Figures in locked suitcases and hit over the head, for example. 'When you improvise, you sometimes take a step too far.' He ends the workshop and asks Des to pass around printouts with breathing guides and dialogue examples. 'Thank you everyone, great work!' Raphael says, as people pack up puppets, whispering.

Raphael wears sunglasses and a Hawaiian shirt. His beard is streaked with grey and over his shoulder is his weekend bag. They're walking through London Bridge station on their way to Eastbourne. He whistles because he loves holidays. Other Esther is silent. Esther's face is wet with tears.

Their pre-booked tickets are released from the machine in a satisfying pile which Raphael pockets. They hover near the seating area when Esther says to Raphael, 'Ask if I'm okay.'

He's distracted, looking for the platform number. 'What's that?'

'Ask if I'm okay.'

'You're okay, Esther.'

'I want you to ask if I'm okay. Why won't you ask?' It's like scratching air, this attempt to communicate with him.

'You're okay. I'm okay. Everything is okay.' He stops outside one of the shops on the concourse. 'I'm going to get something to read for the journey. Do you want to wait here?'

Raphael browses the racks trying to decide between an antique furniture journal and *National Geographic*. He had to take a break from Esther because he doesn't know what to say to her when she's so upset. Maybe they can talk when she's calmed down. He's trying his best. He's only ever tried his best. Besides, who has the strength to hold the weight of grief? People find ways to reshape it, bury it or throw it hard against a wall. He wanders over to other shelves and flicks through a bestseller.

Raphael pays for the antique magazine and a paperback, plus a sudoku book for them all. Outside the shop, Esther is not where he left her. There's a huge crash nearby and he hears cafe staff shout at each other before he sees them. One has dropped a large box of glasses or plates and they both stand around it, yelling. A gritty and burnt smell reaches Raphael's nose and he realises something is wrong. He calls Esther's phone, but it's diverted to voicemail. 'Esther!' he shouts, running towards the escalator. He has the train tickets, but she has the carrycot. People frown in his direction. He shouts, 'Esther!'

Hotels should put clocks in the bathrooms, or else people are at risk of losing any sense of time. Instead, Esther has been stranded in a moment, in a room within a room, one of many rooms on a floor of rooms within a long building filled with other rooms.

Esther stares down at Other Esther, lying there on the bathmat. She's never been so still. It's not possible to know what goes on in people's minds, although sometimes we can guess. We can assume it's around two-thirty a.m. when Esther finds herself on her feet holding Other Esther over the bath. There is a pause, but not a long one. When she drops her, the sound of the splash is like a slap.

She turns around and opens the bathroom door. The pace picks up and she is soon dashing around the bedroom shoving clothes into her backpack. The TV shows a *Tom and Jerry* cartoon. While she zips her jeans, Esther glimpses Jerry's bulging eyes as he's caught in a trap. The speed increases as soon as she abandons the room. Esther sprints along a grey-carpeted corridor, down and around the stairwell, across the too-bright reception, and bursts from the automatic doors onto the pavement.

The traffic glides and sirens sing on King's Cross Road. A man holds a placard as he walks, but Esther is running too fast to see what it says. The air feels thin and fragile around her, as if it is a delicacy to be savoured. She chooses a direction and heads towards Holborn. The sky begins to show signs of the dawn and she slows by a tall red-brick church, which has two round windows looking out over the street. Esther stops and looks up to watch the clouds above form, reform and float away.

My Mother Bred Me for Timidity

The walls were disgusting. If they weren't displaying replica firearms, from pistols to double-barrelled shotguns, it was dead animals. Attached to a wooden plaque was a stuffed buffalo head. Two curved horns, glass eyes and nostrils as big as fists. Willa sat on a bar stool and looked around at Islington's finest glowing in the restaurant's orange light. People were digging into food while wearing oversized glasses and laughing too loudly. Country music cried from many speakers.

While Willa waited for the festival team, the man behind the bar made her a cocktail called 'After the Hunt', smoky and strong. By the time the others arrived, Willa had finished her first drink and was almost done with her second.

'We're so incredibly excited to meet you,' said Carlos the festival director, as Willa shook his damp palm and suffered the larger than necessary silver rings on his fingers. 'The great Willa Breton. I've followed your work for years.' He was no older than thirty.

Willa put her drink on the bar and sighed.

'Right,' said Carlos, with a smile. 'I've brought along our brilliant producer and an exceptional performer in her own right, Han.'

'Oh, stop,' said a young woman with cropped black hair,

like Demi Moore in *Ghost*. She squeezed his arm and looked happy about the comment. They'd both flown in from New York the night before. Han said, 'It's an honour to meet you.' She must have been early twenties, at most, and her accent was Midwestern.

After the air kiss, Willa said, 'I also found an older man useful early in my career.' She'd met a marvellous Argentinian once who softly sang her to sleep. Whatever happened to him?

Meanwhile, Han was talking through her many achievements, backed up by Carlos who said when they met, he recognised her innate talent as well as her determination. Willa nodded along.

Carlos had contacted her agent to say his favourite of her pieces was *Listen to Me if You Want a Good Life*. In the show she performed extracts of her sister's teenage diary with tarantulas crawling across her body. It won two international stage awards some time ago. He'd said he wanted to commission something new, and there was a significant financial offer on the table, but apparently was concerned there wasn't an audience for Willa's style of work anymore. So, here she was, sitting at a bar for the first time in years, with all these young people, having tiresome conversations, all to demonstrate she was still relevant.

'It's colder than usual for January, is it not?' she said.

Han visibly relaxed. This was a topic she could contribute towards. 'My secret is Uniqlo's Heattech. I would absolutely freeze without my Uniqlo leggings, Uniqlo tops, Uniqlo socks.' She leaned in closer. 'Even underwear. It helps regulate body temperature, so when you're outside you're all cosy. Inside, you're cool.'

Willa stepped back. 'Is that so? What I like about winter is that everyone walks around not noticing their noses dripping.' She shook her head. 'Bodies are uncontrollable this time of year.'

As Han and Carlos sipped their drinks quietly another person came bundling through the door wrapped in an enormous jacket. He had face glitter and many bangles on his wrist. It was Armitage, a giant Canadian artist based in London. Willa had met him once before. This time, like last time, she immediately felt plain and lifeless. She glanced down at her dress, which was the colour and shape of a sack. *They shouldn't make clothes in this colour,* she thought.

'Your coat,' Willa said to Armitage.

'Yes. I know. Beaver. I know, I know,' he said. 'But it was my grandmother's and she died last month.'

Willa found herself nodding, as if she understood. 'I'm so sorry,' she said. In her mind, beaver children leapt about on a riverside somewhere, wondering if their dad would ever come home.

Their table was narrow, each place laid with an erect white napkin on top of each plate. To get to his seat, Armitage ducked under the deer antlers protruding from a wooden plaque, several feet long. He grinned the whole time, acting out a boxing fight with the beast. Willa was next to Han. The others were opposite. Carlos took his time rolling up his shirt sleeves, showing tattoos of dragons and roses. Across the internet, people performed their lives and others spent evenings following their trails. For example, pictures from Carlos' wedding were in a photographer's digital gallery and Willa had clicked through every image. The burgundy suit was a risk that paid off. His wife wore a dress in the same colour and long black gloves. The bouquet was a human skull, or a replica of one.

'Walking piece of art, aren't you?' said Willa, knowing Carlos would appreciate the compliment. Then they all talked about London and Willa quoted a line from a Frank O'Hara poem: 'Is it dirty / does it look dirty / that's what you think of in the city.'

Wine was ordered and they explored the menu. The dishes listed in the menu were all rugged, arrogant, masculine. Roasted, seared or smoked. Dry-cured meats, pates and sausages.

'We absolutely have to get the charcuterie board,' Han was saying. 'Or we could have the half-roasted Amish chicken.'

Willa looked at Han. From an online search, Willa knew Han was born in 1998, and had a fun time at the dentist recently. She reviewed the hygienist as 'a good soul' and 'the kind of woman that would be a lifelong friend'. Meanwhile, Carlos was talking about kung fu, and how he and his partner both spent early mornings at the studio, followed by a shared breakfast. Willa drifted off and looked around. The wild boar on the wall had ears pricked, teeth rising up from its bottom jaw and tongue lifted. *I know how you feel,* thought Willa.

Han noticed her looking at the decor. 'I love seeing these animals close up,' she said.

'Yes,' said Willa. 'Shame they're dead.'

Hearing their conversation, Carlos shared some insights. 'I believe hunting is an ancient impulse. It's such a noble skill.'

The others agreed. Armitage said, 'Hunting is actually good for animals, because the landowners start expanding their habitats and protecting them. They start to understand the need for the animals' long-term survival.'

'Is that so?' said Willa. She thought of her own long-term survival. Enough money and an extra soft sofa to sink into at the end of the day.

The waitress arrived and listed the specials.

'Does anyone else feel like tonight's the night we eat Tomahawk steak?' said Carlos. With the mention of meat, he sat upright, like a child.

The steak's flavour was out of this world, the waitress said. Armitage wanted to try it. He was one of the festival's associate artists and a late addition to the party, so Willa had not been able to complete her usual level of internet research.

Han clasped her hands together, delighted. 'I love eating family-style. Reminds me of your piece, Willa. The one with hot sauce that people transferred from their mouths to strangers. Do you mind me mentioning it?'

Willa smiled. She was young, then. It was a lighter version than the original idea, which involved sauce on genitals. Her agent encouraged her to focus on pieces where pain was fleeting, followed swiftly by hope and relief. But why bother making art if you didn't force people to see people as they actually were?

Eating spicy food released the same level of endorphins as vigorous exercise, Armitage was saying, naming a study he'd read.

Carlos said he was impressed at Armitage's knowledge, then guided everyone back to the menu. 'So is that three, four of us? Willa?' His tone was so friendly.

Willa said nothing. She waited. The waitress hovered, topping up already full water glasses.

Armitage grabbed Willa's shoulder. 'God, I just thought. You're not vegetarian, are you?'

Carlos took a swig of wine. 'Imagine never tasting meat. How would you know if you liked it or not?'

Willa could predict all that followed. It started with a story leading to a complaint:

'My sister's new girlfriend is vegetarian,' said Carlos, fiddling with his napkin. 'For the holidays, my folks cooked all vegetarian foods to make her feel welcome. It didn't feel like Christmas to me.'

Then the concern:

'I'm so sorry,' said Armitage. 'And I want to know where the hell they get their protein from?'

Followed by accusation:

'We didn't know.' Han flashed her eyes at Carlos, then at Willa. 'If we'd have known… we assumed, with the tarantulas…'

'Mechanical,' said Willa.

'You're wearing leather shoes, darling,' said Armitage.

Willa lifted her foot above the table. 'Vegan.'

Han touched her hair, flattening it down then puffing it up, and grinning oddly. 'Well, there will definitely be something you can eat.'

Willa looked around the table and felt outnumbered. She wanted this commission. She said, 'Eating meat. It's not something I understand,' as if her only concern was comprehension.

'Right,' said Armitage. 'I can explain. It tastes good.' He mimed chewing on the most delicious food imaginable.

The waitress had drifted away, but they called her back.

'We'll take the steak,' said Armitage.

'You're not offended are you, Willa?' Han said. 'I can eat the vegetarian food too. They can keep the meat at the far end of the table.'

'It's such a special occasion tonight,' said Carlos. 'I barely eat meat, except when I see something like this on the menu.'

'The caramelised sprouts here are nice,' said the waitress.

'Good,' said Carlos. 'Let's take steak, and a load of vegetarian side dishes.' He also asked the waitress to bring more wine.

'Talking of food, in my next piece, I had an idea to employ ballet dancers to perform in a chocolate fountain,' said Armitage.

Han said it sounded amazing. Her cheeks were flushed.

Willa said, 'Perhaps the women would then be asked to dance semi-naked, covering the audience or a wall or the floor in dripping chocolate trails?'

Armitage nodded, not picking up on her tone. 'How beautiful to see rich chocolate fall like raindrops from the delicious bodies of the performers.'

Willa felt tired. She resorted to a phrase she had used many times before. 'You've always been someone interested in pushing boundaries.'

Armitage reached out for her hand and said he knew she would understand. From then on, the meal seemed dull and pointless to Willa. She sat back in her chair. Everything any of them said was unremarkable. Beneath the stuffed head of an ibex with almond-shaped eyes, a family of four forked egg dishes and sausages into their mouths. The ibex had silvery fur and its head was turned to the left, quizzical. *Where do they hide the shot marks?* thought Willa.

'Why don't you come closer?' said Han at one point.

Willa shuffled her chair towards the table. The waitress set down steak knives by each plate except her own.

'What are you thinking?' asked Han, trying to open a separate conversation, aside from the other two.

'I was looking at the animals on the wall,' said Willa. 'Do you think people would still hunt so eagerly if they weren't allowed to take the head or the horns or the body as a trophy?'

Han said, 'The thrill of the chase is most important. It's primitive. We used to bring down mammoths.'

'All humans are driven by ego. We need to assert power over animals, over people, over everything.'

'Well, look.' Han flicked through her phone. 'It says here, some species need to be kept under control. Elephants destroy land, pulling at trees, ravishing fields. They are killed for the safety of the village.' She continued scrolling and reading, then frowned. She didn't share the rest of the piece.

Willa said, 'Do you like London? Will you have time to explore?'

'I wish! It's meetings, meetings, meetings.'

'I see.' Willa told a story about one of her impromptu pieces, the sort that made her name. She'd taken a ceramics course at her local adult education college. In the main hall, at the end of term show, Willa walked to the display and threw each pot against the wall. As she did, she called out the names of old, lost friends. There were many. She enjoyed the shattering sound and left only three or four pieces intact by the time they restrained her. The twelve Polaroid photographs taken by her assistant were displayed in an exhibition called *The Cracks in my*

Life. Each was now worth a bit of money, although none had been sold.

Han listened and said all the right things. When Carlos involved himself in their conversation, he said he was excited to be potentially supporting Willa to create new work. Willa said she was excited to be potentially supported by them to create it. Everyone laughed.

When the waitress brought over the steak, steaming in its tray, Carlos, Han and Armitage looked so pleased, as if they'd won a prize. The aroma in the air was sticky and sweet.

'I literally cannot wait,' said Armitage.

Han lifted her plate, ready for Carlos to carve and serve. At that moment, a table of friends began to sing happy birthday. Armitage joined in but directed his song to the steak, replacing 'birthday' with 'death day'.

As the song concluded Willa reached for one of the steak knives, thrust back her chair and fell to her knees. She stuck out her tongue and extended it over a plate. Knife poised on the flesh, she lisped, 'Dare me?'

It was not the clearest articulation, but they understood. Voices around them quietened.

'What are you doing?' Carlos said, looking from side to side.

Willa pressed the tip of the knife onto her tongue, beginning to taste blood. She knew this was not the cleverest of her improvised pieces, but she meant every movement.

Carlos stood up and clapped. 'Ladies and gentlemen,' he called. 'We are witnessing the unveiling of the new Willa Breton.'

There were murmurs around the room. Of course, she was not famous enough for people to know who she was, even the strenuously cool kids who ate at an East London early American-style restaurant. Still, a few cheered.

'What's going on?' asked Armitage.

The waitress rushed over but then stopped nearby, unsure. 'Should I call someone?'

'No, no,' said Carlos. 'She's performing.'

Willa grunted. She always found it interesting how rapidly people began to talk about her as soon as she did anything unexpected.

Carlos looked around. 'Is someone filming? Is someone filming her? Han?'

But Han was fixed to the spot.

'The body as pure object,' said Armitage, from behind his iPhone. 'The camera on this is excellent.'

'We share in her agony as if her hurt is our hurt,' said Carlos.

Willa drew the knife across her tongue one way then the other, creating a cross. There would be no blood drops, only a bubbling line of red her saliva would soon dilute and wash down her throat.

'I just want to say that if this is about the steak, the meat has been cooked now. It'll go to waste,' called Armitage.

Willa felt some pain, as she had during the research of this work. She changed the angle of the knife and let it rest on the tip of her tongue, before moving it back and forth, like a metronome.

There were screams. *People really are too sentimental,* Willa thought. Besides, the tongue was tougher than people knew. The blade barely made an impact, only there was a thick sensation in Willa's mouth.

'Are you getting this?' called Carlos to Armitage.

Other diners began to turn in their seats. Willa could see Carlos nearby, standing with his decorated arms folded. He was the one who made final decisions on work they commissioned. What was he thinking? When she dug the knife in deeper, people shrieked.

'My god!' Armitage had a hand over his chest but was still filming.

Willa's head felt slow, yet she was focused. It was always this way when she performed: inhabiting the moment and living in it. Movement stilled. Simply her and her body and a deep, mineral happiness. She was close to her essential being, and to all humankind and the wider world.

Then there was a rush nearby and Han's hand was on Willa's arm. 'Please don't,' she whispered beside her. 'I'm sorry about this evening. I really am sorry, but don't do this.'

Han's arm was around her now, and Willa saw red stains on the bare skin. Noises reduced to a low hum. No one had ever joined her during a performance.

Han touched a napkin near Willa's mouth. 'I think the piece is provocative. Really it is. Beautiful in many ways, so beautiful. Your body, just there. Being. But I can't enjoy it if I think you're in pain. It doesn't feel right. It's not right. I'm sorry.'

Willa concentrated on her breathing and said, with some difficulty, 'I can take the pain.'

Han stroked her hair for a while and then said. 'Yeah, but why should you?'

Willa's mother bred her to be timid and quiet like a woman should be, so Willa found a way to claim space. Once she'd hung herself from a giant hook. For *Skittle*, she stood in a bowling alley letting people throw heavy balls towards her feet until the ambulance came, and the police.

Willa slid the steak knife from her tongue and placed it on the table. People gasped, then began to clap. Armitage wolf whistled. The applause kept coming. There was cheering. A camera flashed and there was a rising sound of excited chatter. Willa looked at Han and stood slowly. What she had inside her was a new feeling. She took the bloody napkin and raised it high to her audience.

What Would You Have Said?

In Casey Carpenters' first all-staff meeting he says he sees his role as facilitator rather than leader. Although it is a cool February morning, his shirt is unbuttoned at the collar as well as the two buttons below. He has short, neat hair. People sip coffee and pick at croissants as he speaks. The meeting takes place on the upper floor, which has many windows looking onto Clerkenwell sky and honey-coloured buildings. It's a good room, but hot. There are two shelves filled with potted plants, all of which have spent too long in the sun. Leaves slowly turn brown, soil turns to dust.

Casey's vision for the company is to empower staff. He wants to bring the company into the twenty-first century. There are questions he wants the whole company to answer together. What needs a revamp? Where are the opportunities? How can they change the workplace for the better? Casey holds out his hands to the room. People come first, he says.

The room chatters and employees soon call out ideas. A weekly happy hour! Karaoke room! Bring your pet to work day! A woman called Bo Fielding takes a different approach: she wants a staff representative at director-level meetings. Her hair is long and grey, pinned high on her head, and one strand from the front falls down as she speaks. Casey promises he will consider all proposals. Diane Davies takes notes in a reporter's pad. She seems to be holding her breath. Casey says Diane will design suggestion boxes and create a dedicated email address. He wants each person to contribute and crazy proposals are super welcome. Freedom to share thoughts is freedom to take risks, which is freedom to succeed.

In the next month's meeting, Casey greets everyone with his palms pressed in a gesture of prayer. His hair has grown and now curls above and around his head. From the window, soft buds on the tree branches show signs of early spring. After some preliminary remarks, decisions are announced. Casual Friday is a popular proposal. He is thrilled to agree a relaxed dress code and four p.m. office wind-down to close the week. People clap at the news. A small caveat: could he ask directors to feedback on this policy with regard to meeting deadlines? Casey also approves a rejuvenated staff recognition scheme, fresh fruit each day in the shared kitchens, and a karaoke night on the last Thursday of each month. The atmosphere fizzes as people talk and laugh with colleagues.

Casey holds up his hand for attention as he wants to share the fourth idea. He clears his throat, looks around the room, then says he is excited to introduce Quiet Wednesdays. Casey says this proposal included a ten-point implementation plan and a supplementary document on how office noise pollution impacts on staff wellbeing and physical health. Among us, he says, is an individual seeking and not yet finding their optimum working environment. You should be able to bring your full self to work and if one person wants a day of quiet in their working week, others must want a day of quiet too.

Gemma Seltzer

Immediately, there are questions and many people fold their arms. They are unhappy because quiet is not in their nature. It is simply a trial, says Casey, and he will listen to feedback. They want to know how they will brainstorm. How will actions be agreed? If they have something to say, why not say it? It's stuffy in the room, but the windows are double-glazed and sealed shut. The air conditioning should regulate the space soon. Casey wants them to spend a moment reframing their anger. Can they welcome change and not give in to fear? Could everyone support an anonymous colleague and embark on this new journey? After further discussion, the majority relax, and a few admit they are intrigued. Plus, this is a good company with excellent benefits. Staff return to their desks speaking to each other a great deal.

The Quiet Wednesday policy is shared and states that while emails can continue and instant messages too, the aim is not to increase non-verbal communication, but reduce the volume of all communication. Adding reflective pauses before taking action increases both productivity and wellbeing. Quiet Wednesdays are non-hierarchical, and people are responsible for the success of the idea.

The next Wednesday, people try to be quiet from the moment they enter the building. The hallways are filled with the sound of giggling and exaggerated 'shush' sounds. Everyone knows there should be no chatting, but high fives are okay. There are many of them. Morning chitchat within teams is not allowed, although colleagues with good working relationships place a hand on each other's shoulder in greeting. Phones should be on silent, with calls diverted to a message stating enquiries will be answered the following day.

Soon, the number of employees pacing back and forth in corridors giving opinions into mobile phones dwindles. By the water fountain, people stand quietly and wait their turn. Training days help staff practise being quiet in short bursts to build up stamina.

One unexpected outcome is people choose to bring slippers to work, because of the looks received when they dash around in heels or squeaky leather shoes. Now mid-morning on Wednesdays the only sounds are the low purr of air conditioning and the tiny chink of porcelain as someone stirs tea.

It is not those who talk the loudest that are promoted, but the quiet ones. All staff meetings now begin and close with ten minutes' silent contemplation on the week before, then the week ahead. In the human resources area, the walls are painted pale blue. The director has established a jigsaw table and people add sections to a thousand-piece puzzle throughout the day. A product designer joins the comms officer to host workshops on the relationship between words and image. Staff learn to craft speeches and presentations while considering visual impact, rhythm and progression. PowerPoints soon burst with images and the light voiceover is emotive and precise. The designer and comms officer now attend senior management team meetings.

Staff look forward to Quiet Wednesdays and express pride that they work for such an innovative company. Despite challenging financial times, they feel the company is investing in its people.

Gemma Seltzer

Bo Fielding does not believe Quiet Wednesdays are good for the company. On Mondays, Tuesdays, Thursdays and Fridays, she is sure to mention her relief it's not Quiet Wednesday. She says this to anyone who passes her desk, those who she sees in the kitchen and to her clients on calls.

Bo likes to have an opinion on everything from the shape of door handles to how best to wear a blouse. She listens to the news and podcasts all evening and into the night. Bo always asks people for specific details. Which carriage were they in when the train was delayed? What were they wearing? How would they describe the atmosphere and what would it mean if it were a metaphor?

In the AOB section of one particular meeting, Bo lists her concerns. It is a Monday and she makes the most of it. She says she feels her projects are progressing too slowly because people have stopped communicating updates. They've effectively lost a day of work because so many people use Quiet Wednesdays to think rather than *do* anything. As she speaks, Bo organises some leftover handouts into a rough pile. Her nails are painted dark red. Her dress is cobalt blue. She says, shouldn't they *do* something?

Diane is in this meeting with six others, including the head of finance, a nice woman with wavy hair and dimples. No one answers Bo but they do look around at each other. Diane makes notes on her pad.

Bo says she'll happily keep talking until someone answers. She says the hardest working member of her team has been overlooked for a new role. As feedback, the panel mentioned his expressive voice, and wondered whether it might intimidate clients. Unfortunately, he interrupted an interviewer while she was speaking. It was suggested he should look for a job outside the company. What do you think of that? Bo waits for a response.

This top floor room really is one of the nicest areas of the building, as the long windows frame the mid to upper section of eucalyptus trees, like a camera shot. The bark is reddish and smooth, flaking in places and bright in the sunshine. The leaves of the tree sway. Those who are lucky enough to sit on the table's far side look to the window. Some shuffle in their chairs for a better view.

The head of finance eventually says maybe Bo shouldn't worry so much.

My god, shouts Bo. She is older than many of them. What has happened to you all? This is going to go very wrong. I'm sure of it. We have to do something. Don't you realise, she says, while drawing angry moustaches on the handout's cover photograph as she talks, that Casey has all the power here?

People whisper responses. They have other concerns in their lives, so appreciate the calm atmosphere at work. Many are going through things. Some are going through bereavements. Some through house moves. Another recently through a life change: he has returned from paternity leave. No one wants to lose their job.

The door swings open and a woman from the data team enters with a singing bowl. She skates a wooden mallet around the edge, and it fills the room with its gentle sound.

This is bullshit, says Bo, slamming the table.

Diane looks down at her pad. The head of finance sighs and shakes her head.

Bo leaves early that day, packing up her bag angrily. When she is in the lift, she growls at the notice for a five rhythms class. The image is of a single person, dancing alone. Bo leans forward and rips the paper from its tape. She marches down Farringdon Lane towards the station, outraged at her colleagues. She'd seen so many managers and directors, chief executives and trustees come and go. Still, no one listened to her. Who were all these people wasting time outside the Betsy Trotwood? Laughing their heads off, pints swishing in their hands.

The green man flashes as she approaches Clerkenwell Road and Bo is pleased she can cross straight away so her thoughts keep on track. She's sure Casey has other motives. He's a man, after all. The history of mankind is silencing womankind. A pair of gulls shriek overhead. She needs a few allies, then they can begin their offensive. She'll talk to her sister on the phone this evening, and maybe a few friends. Then, she decides, after she's cooked dinner for everyone, put the kids to bed, and gone through it with her husband a couple of times, she'll do some research online.

Outside the tube entrance, a man with a briefcase is in her path. He faces her and has a full head of dark hair with a matching dark beard. As she moves to the left, he does too. She shifts right, and there he is again. Then he steps back and laughs, and gestures ahead. Please, he says. Fine, Bo replies. She feels him smiling after her as she walks away but she doesn't look back.

It's life, isn't it? This give and take, the please and thank you, the it's my turn, it's your turn. Bo slams her phone on the card reader, her blood racing around her body as she thumps down the stairs to the train.

Diane Davies does not think Quiet Wednesdays are bullshit. It's the other days she dislikes. Her desk faces Bo's and both are outside Casey's office. Bo shops at the weekends and presents herself to Diane in bright, new clothes on Monday mornings. It has been this way since Diane began working here. Three months after that Diane bought a dimmer switch for her bedroom and spent her evenings under the bulb's calm half-light.

After the recent meeting, Bo has been pushing Diane to agree with her. Bo has even followed her into the toilets to let her know the company is bad. Would she join them to end Casey's tyranny?

On this day, the following Monday, Bo has her hands on her hips. What do you think? she asks. She has a burgundy long-sleeved jumpsuit. Was it right for work?

Diane pauses over her keyboard. She arrived early to finish these notes, and she's almost there. Between their desks is a pile of folders, so Diane has to stretch her neck to look at Bo. She acknowledges her and says the jumpsuit is really nice. Bo wants her to stand so she can see properly, but Diane says she can see fine. Bo flaps her wrist to beckon Diane and says she doesn't have all day. Continuing to type, Diane asks if she can look later, but Bo goes on and on. Diane reaches for her keyboard, saves her document, and slowly stands. Now she has Diane's full attention, Bo embarks on a story about the first market stall in Spitalfields Market where the owner kept staring at her chest, so he got no business from her and she reported him as well. The second stall had these jumpsuits—

Diane cuts in and says she looks really great. She sits back down.

Gemma Seltzer

I wish I could concentrate as well as you at work, Bo says. She wishes she didn't have so many ideas sprinting around in her mind. She wishes she could stop joining other people's meetings and pitches, but she knows her expertise is invaluable. She'd have time to sit at her desk all day, like Diane. Bo says staff really need to rally together against the oppressive Quiet Wednesday regime. It's curbing their freedoms. She is whispering now and says she's organising a meeting for everyone who feels silenced.

Diane fixes her face in an expression of attentiveness, while her eyes flash at her screen. Growing up, Diane's favourite activity was visiting the mobile library. Up the metal steps she'd go, holding her mother's hand. The children's section had shelves and a book box. All the books had plastic jackets, some smart, some ragged. Diane would turn the rotating book stand, searching for the best book covers. With a pile of titles, she would sit inside and read. There were other children, and parents, all in there and reading. The library parked outside the big Sainsbury's each fortnight, and there were two librarians. One who stayed inside and talked about the new books, and the other who patrolled the vehicle to prevent kids jamming sharp objects into its wheels. This weekend, Diane saw a mobile library van stuck in traffic on Essex Road. It was a strange sight because there were libraries all over London, although maybe there were children who couldn't visit them. That was what she wanted to say to Bo. That the mobile library meant something to her and so does Quiet Wednesday, but she hasn't yet found the right words.

It doesn't matter. Bo has found another topic of interest and is lecturing her on the value of menstrual cups over tampons. Casey appears from his office and he asks Diane for the meeting minutes. Are they done yet? They aren't. She needs to send them to the chairman for sign off. Casey asks if she wouldn't mind sitting down and saving the chitchat for lunchtime as he did say he needed them before ten.

Diane nods and reaches her fingers towards the keyboard.

Whoopsie, says Bo.

It feels like someone has thrown a soaking wet bath towel over Diane's head. She sits, pulls on her headphones, and rapidly types. As she does, she calms down and begins enjoying her thoughts as they arise. If she could live in one book which would it be? Bo waves at one point for her attention, but Diane keeps her eyes on her screen. She feels her tongue swell in her mouth, sore, dry and blissfully unused. A few times she looks out the window at the sweeping, silent sky. Where were the starlings flying so urgently?

Diane leaves the office while Bo is in a meeting. She heads through the park to Exmouth Market, where she waves at colleagues who cycle by. As she passes Café Kick, she sees two men concentrating on their table football game. One rotates the pole gently, as if it is a precious thing, then rolls and catches it again. The ball hits one side and his friend cheers. On the steps of Finsbury Town Hall, a girl in white tights and a matching leotard is standing with her mother, a balloon tied to her wrist. Diane follows her usual route along Upper Street via the supermarket and then home to her house share behind Highbury and Islington station. She pauses in the hallway when she arrives. There are no sounds except the steady click of the kitchen clock. The others will return from work soon, and then there will be music and footsteps, saucepans and frying smells.

Gemma Seltzer

Dashing upstairs to her room, she unpacks her bags and puts them away. She returns her shoes to the designated place in the wardrobe. Diane has her plates, cutlery and a kettle in a crate on a low table. She's in for the night. One good feature of her bedroom is a sink, and above it: an ornate mirror with metal flowers covering each edge. Diane stares at her face for a long time. After a while, she smiles.

At the next all-staff meeting, the usual coffee carts are there and it's black americanos people order. Casey now combs his hair to one side, letting it flick up and over his right ear. He sits on a table, swinging his legs back and forth. Welcome, he says, as people enter. Diane is nearby, notepad poised.

It's the end of summer now. The eucalyptus trees' red bark glows in the daylight. All the windows in the building opposite are swung open. Staff can see people moving about behind the glass, brushing their teeth and drying their hair while looking out to the day. In this office, the air conditioning continues to hum.

Casey says he feels more positive than ever. Revenue is up and he's seen productivity rise markedly on Wednesdays. The recent directors' report say projects are being delivered on time if not early, and previously less visible staff members are producing exceptionally high-quality work. There is a soft, spontaneous round of applause and those who recently received promotions grin and shrug. I think we're onto something, he says, I think we've found our secret sauce. We are the right company in the right moment to take advantage of this discovery. We can transform ourselves, and the world. Casey wants them to move to a new phase. They'll be doubling down on the quiet idea. Now, every day will be quiet!

Some people clap but anger rises immediately from a group sitting together near the front of the room. One woman hurls her coffee cup to the ground, and lets the dark liquid trail over the floorboards. Bo Fielding is on her feet. She is wearing high-waisted trousers and thick-heeled brogues. See, see! she shouts, pointing at Casey and then at people in the room. I knew it! I knew you had bigger plans. I knew you wanted to stop us from speaking out. But we will not be silenced. She starts clapping and chanting: We will not be silenced.

A few others join in and the clapping gets louder, but most people look on quietly. Diane finds the loose thread on her sleeve occupies her attention for a while.

Hold on, hold on! says Casey. Our company has the chance to be a sector leader.

The woman who threw the coffee cup cries into her hands.

Casey raises his voice. It's pretty dramatic to say this is about silencing. The rise in revenue over the last few months speaks for itself. We all want to see the company succeed, don't we?

Bo wants to know where the evidence is that a quiet office is a better office? Is he willing to share the reports from directors?

Of course, of course, says Casey, but he doesn't look anyone in the eye.

The meeting dissolves into low-voiced conversations. Bo and her group hurry out of the room. Diane and a few others drift towards the windows. They see people on the pavement below hurrying and holding shopping bags. When Diane returns to her desk, Bo is typing vigorously. She has her mouth pressed shut.

By mid-morning the atmosphere across the office is muted and there have been many arguments. On the second floor, a man continued talking loudly into his phone when warned to stop. A strange smell alerted people to a burned slipper in the kitchen.

At lunchtime, Bo pushes back her chair and heads to a central point on the floor, just near the lifts. Simultaneously, eight or nine people walk towards the same point. When they reach each other they start to scream. They scream together, a horrible high-pitched unbroken sound as if none of them any longer need to breathe.

They scream with eyes open but not focusing on any specific thing. They scream in an endless howl, shaking their heads and raising hands to the ceiling. They scream as their arms are held and the security guards escort them from the building.

Staff rush upstairs to the top floor for a view out of the windows. They jostle for positions to see the group on the pavements outside. While they look down, the others stare up to the sealed shut office windows, their mouths still open and screaming.

The quiet office gathers momentum. Staff feature in magazines about the unique company culture and their stories are shared on LinkedIn. They are interviewed and say they didn't imagine they'd ever be able to think so clearly.

Diane pursues tasks effectively and meets deadlines. She is given more management responsibilities and now oversees the internal engagement programme. It seems obvious to her now, the idea of quiet workplaces. She is developing her original concept into a website and she's absolutely sure it will resonate with people all across the world. When she passes her colleagues in the corridors, they nod, as if all of them are holy and holding private, important knowledge. So, as the world outside keeps on shouting, Diane's days in the office slip by, quiet and good.

The top floor meeting room has been transformed into a meditation space, with soft mats and piles of folded blankets. Printers are used much less, and plants tended more. The Christmas cactus bursts into bloom one weekend, and they arrive on Monday morning to see it filled with so many tubular hot pink flowers.

Gemma Seltzer

Ways of Living

Two women sitting on a train and one turns to the other and says, 'This is our stop. I recognise the notices on the platform.'

One, Colette, says, 'No. There are quite a few to go. You're confused. They put up the same advertisement posters in all the stations.' There's spite, or the suggestion of it, here.

'So says you,' says Rose. She has a habit of pulling at her nose repeatedly and does this now.

Colette has watched Rose rub her face in this way for over sixty years. She turns away to think. More often than not, she returns to one significant moment in her life: sitting on a low wall on Bournemouth seafront alongside a man she'd just met, wind whipping their cheeks. In a cafe earlier that day, he had dropped his newspaper, which she'd picked up from the floor. He suggested a walk outside. They'd spoken so softly they could barely hear each other.

'Café Rouge,' Rose is saying.

That's the name of the restaurant they'll eat lunch at, to celebrate the birthday of Rose's son Jack. In her lap, Colette holds a street map, a single sheet of paper marked with their destination. The tips of her index fingers are white with the pressure of touch. She says, 'We can walk to Covent Garden from Blackfriars. It'll be nice, a bit longer but we can go by the river.'

'Let's get a bus,' replies Rose. 'Unless you forgot your pass again?'

Colette says, 'I have it. I just prefer to walk.'

'Fine,' says Rose. 'But I'm getting the bus. Do what you want.'

The anger comes hard to Colette, jagged and black. Other feelings compete for attention. Envy watching Rose marry in ivory silk aged nineteen. Bitterness when Rose's first baby was called the healthiest on the ward. Desperation as life floated by while Colette sat exams and read newspapers. Then, like caught food slowly sliding down your throat, the moment eases. Because Colette was once courted with poetry and flowers. She'll never forget. She was twenty-four when Rose's brother Ernest stood at her door with a fresh shave and shined shoes. It was all rather embarrassing really, but also rather too short. She remembers rolling her toe over the doorstep and thinking, *Remember this.* Awkwardness gave way to a sort of familiar intimacy and then there was a synagogue wedding, two children, the days upon days, and the spare room in which she spent hours studying photographs of herself and her family, tracing the thick brows of the men and the women's jaws.

The train holds its passengers outside Mill Hill Broadway for a moment, as the two women hear each other's opinions on the rain slicing against the window. Rose's gratification that her washing was not on the line that morning, regret from Colette that hers was. And all the while a growing sense of anticipation heightened by the sodden landscape. The haze lifts, the train moves. It's clear again.

People get on and off; the doors wheeze open each time. Rose and Colette smile at a man who sits opposite. He is smart in a pinstriped suit but there's something of a teenager about him. Slouching, chewing gum. At his stop, he vaults

Gemma Seltzer

from the seat with great urgency. A chocolate bar wrapper, a Twix, remains on the seat. Both women lean forward but Colette is there first and leans over to tuck it into the rubbish bin, letting the lid snap as it shuts.

Rose says, 'When I was first a mother, I used to have terrible moments in the night.'

'Wind, you mean?' Colette gazes at the man advancing along the platform, intent now, umbrella swinging.

'No!' Rose laughs. 'No!'

Colette smiles.

Serious now, Rose says, 'I used to find myself on my feet before I was fully awake because Jack was crying.'

Caught between listening and charting their progress on the train, Colette sees herself as a young woman. Aged eighteen, remembered from one of the photographs and she was blond, grinning into the distance, unaware she was under the lens. That was around the time the man from Bournemouth went away. It took her a very long time to understand she'd never see him again. Then, locked in a white photo frame, in her thirties, she's having a picnic with friends; her dress has slipped above her knees, one of the men looks on keenly. Early fifties, grey-haired, sensible shoes, with her brooding husband, hair parted on one side, gripping her hand.

Rose says, 'It was wild. Like a passion. I would have killed for him.'

'Maternal instinct, they call it,' Colette replies. 'I had it too.'

But Rose's memory is only for herself. 'Not the same way.'

Colette twists the skin on her wrist as far as it will go, to make sure she does still have skin, that it reacts when touched, that it responds to pressure. When she releases, a purple depression remains, and she's elated. *Still here, then.*

A woman nearby is trying to manoeuvre her buggy between a suitcase and a series of rigid legs. Colette smiles at the child strapped in, opening and closing its fists. 'Hello,' she says. 'Hello, hello.' The sun shines as bright as egg yolk now, and the air in the train is warm.

Rose's eyes are on the mother as she continues loudly, 'They move on and have their own families. They forget about you.'

Colette thinks Rose goes on about her life too much. She says, 'Which station is this?'

'Those nights, I'd be on my feet and ready to give myself fully to this tiny baby.' Rose pauses and looks intently out of the window. 'West Hampstead.'

Colette says, 'We've got plenty of time to get there. Let's walk to Covent Garden.'

Rose gathers her handbag to her chest. 'The bus is fine for me.'

Two women sitting on a train and one turns to the other and says, 'Is she nice, Gabriella? His wife?'

Rose says, 'She's nice. Yes.'

This news pleases Colette. It is possible that people can have years of happiness together. In Ernest's letters, he said his secret to living well was her, was love. That was good, she always thought.

Rose says, 'She makes terrible cakes. Floury. No jam in the middle, but miniature flowers lining the edge. She picks them from the garden and puts them on the cakes!'

Gemma Seltzer

Colette thinks that's a strange thing to criticise. She says, 'We could have a snack somewhere before we find the bus. The party starts at three, so we'd have time.'

'We can have tea if we must, but nothing to eat.'

'Tea?' Colette considers this.

'She has a temper though, I've seen it,' Rose says. 'Why Jack puts up with it, I don't know.'

Colette's fingers reach for her wrist again. She's never met anyone so sure of herself as Rose. When they were girls, Rose rolled her socks down to her ankles and tore the ribbons from her hair. With surnames beside each other in the alphabet, they were paired in almost every class. Rose liked to talk. All the time. Name a topic, and she had an opinion. She couldn't stop, even when teachers loomed over her and letters were sent home. Colette's only power in those days was to escape into her own body. It started with averting her eyes, sending her thoughts to her toes, letting her hair fall over her face. She resisted being noticed. Even with her own children, she continued this habit, watchful and careful to laugh when things were funny and flatten her mouth when they weren't.

Rose has more to say about her daughter-in-law. 'He must remember how she used to be. Ten years is a long time.'

'It is,' replies Colette. 'I was married for forty-five.'

'So? We had fifty-one happy years.'

Another photograph, this time of the garden in summer. When Ernest died, Colette dug honeysuckle into the edges of the grass. Returning from a month with her daughter, she found the vine had clambered across the entire fence. It sprouted white and pink flowers that filled the air with its sweet smell. How deceptively pleasant the natural world can seem, when survival was all that mattered. From her kitchen window, she would look out and think, *Nature*. There was only Nature. Like here on the train, there was only Now. Like a kick in the chest. Now. Keep moving, tidy, eat, put things in order, while the world around you dies, and lives, and dies again. She never returned to Bournemouth.

Colette says, 'We had some good times, didn't we?'

'I did.'

'So did I.'

'You never seemed to,' replies Rose. 'You always seemed fed up.'

She says, 'I can't have done. Not all the time.'

'I don't know why you even bothered leaving the house. Such a sour face to show the world.'

'Not true.' Colette sighs. She is overwhelmed by a dull sensation of inevitability, the sheer power of sameness, that nothing ever changes, that Rose was Rose, would always be Rose. Whatever anyone thinks of her life and her marriage, she has Ernest's letters in a shoebox with whole sections underlined because they were lovely. With him, she had a daughter and a son. Babies that overwhelmed her with their smell and their growls, meant more to her than she could explain. For them, she felt a throbbing, moist love; so intense she often wondered if she should consider it love at all. Through her husband's moods and his boiling anger, she kept those early letters and poems. A reminder she was once desired.

Colette looks out the window as they pass by Hendon and says, 'It's amazing some of the dates of these buildings. The ones that have stood through the wars.'

Gemma Seltzer

But Rose is too ingrained in the dense earth of her own opinions be uprooted. 'I remember one time when I walked straight out the front door and didn't come home for a night because Alf had shouted at me for burning a hole in his shirt with the iron.' Her bag falls over from a sudden jolt of the train. She shifts forward in her chair and tugs it back onto her lap. 'I went back. Slept on it and came home the next day.' Rose puts a tissue to her nose and gives a hard blow. 'I couldn't go through life not showing how I felt.'

Two women sitting on a train and one turns to the other and says, 'We'd better be getting off soon.'

The other checks her map and replies, 'Two more stops.' She has white hair, candyfloss on her head. Colette never believed she would look like this. She's met a man. She met him at her book group. His name is Sanderson and he is American. When they first spoke, she had two distinct thoughts: There's a tiny mole on his hand I would very much like to touch. And second, Is it possible I've never felt like this before? He uses his mobile phone to send her text messages. Words he writes, just for her, ending each message with a row of three Xs, neatly spaced. She loves that. She's seventy-five next week.

'I want to look in a Marks and Spencer's while we're up in town,' says Rose. 'I like the big stores, where I can get everything I need in one place.'

'What do you need?'

Rose shrugs. 'You know, Gabrielle has no interest in the children.'

Colette says, 'Surely not.'

'She never makes a noise.'

As a child, Colette wished to be older and often wondered how to crease her skin. Have I ever really been loved in all my life? she wonders. 'What sort of noise?'

'Cooing.' Rose draws out the first vowels.

The carriage has filled up. Colette replies, 'Ah.'

Rose snorts as she laughs. 'Yes, a bit like that.'

Colette doesn't believe she was particularly funny. In the reflection, her features seem to be slipping down her face. The glass of the window shows her nose hooking under itself, her eyes sagging. She sees Rose's image beside her. It's something at least, to have known someone for so long. Time seems solid when you have a companion.

'She never shows any sentimentality about her children. Puts their pictures in the bin if there's no room on the fridge, that sort of thing.' Rose tuts. 'They'll take the rejection to adulthood.'

A neat set of terraced houses fill the view from the window. 'Look at those dresses hanging on the washing line,' says Colette, pointing. 'They look like women dangling in the breeze.'

'What?'

'Like a row of women.' She prods her finger into the distance. Sanderson enjoys comments like this. He says she should have been an artist, with her eye for detail and sensitivity to the world. What would she create? Maybe she'd paint. She'd show green fields with speckled sunlight and tiny lambs bleating into the new world, and then slap layers of soupy liquorice black paint over the canvas.

Rose picks at her sleeve. 'I'm not going to the party.' She stares at the door.

Gemma Seltzer

'It'll be fine. The kids will be so pleased to see you.'

'They don't know who I am!'

'Of course they do,' says Colette, softly. 'They adore you.' She's on the periphery of a memory she can't quite place. She sees another photograph. It's blurry but it looks like her and Ernest again, with their daughter. His finger touches the baby's head. Colette tries to experience the sensation she would have felt at the time, but it's too distant. She longs for everything she didn't have then. Rose says, 'Why is she even throwing him this party? She's trying to prove something to me.'

'It's his birthday. It's for him.'

'I only want him to be happy,' Rose says.

'"There are only two happinesses in life, to love and be loved."'

'What's that?'

Colette lets herself smile. 'Nothing. I don't know. Just a line from a letter I had once.'

'Who from?'

'Ernest, of course.' She feels herself blush.

'Oh those!'

'Yes, those.' Colette pauses. Then, 'What do you mean "those"?'

Rose pulls at her nose. '"Your charming eyes," and all that? Well, of course you know he never wrote them.'

Colette's heart begins to skip faster.

'We had such fun putting those together. Reading poetry, finding the right lines to use.'

Colette pauses, searching her mind for clues on this matter. It can't be true.

'I knew you would fall for it. You were such a romantic,'

says Rose. 'We couldn't bear for any more time to pass with you moping about that other man.'

Colette makes a sound like a hum.

'I should be happy my son has married. Some people never do.'

A sense of loss. But Colette can't consider it. She finds some words. 'You said "we"?'

Rose says, 'My sisters! It's funny now, isn't it? What with him being dead for so many years now.'

'Funny?'

'Ernest was better than nothing, wasn't he?' replies Rose. She glances at Colette.

Colette remembers how Ernest always greeted her: with a kiss on her cheek, a neutral and warm slice of contact. He never would read her the letters, even though she asked. Things always find a way of making sense eventually.

Two women sitting on a train and one turns to the other and says, 'This is the longest journey of my life.'

'It *is* taking a while,' says Colette.

Rose folds her arms across her chest. 'I wish we could open the window.' She scans the carriage to see if anyone responds. 'It's amazing how they can't regulate the air conditioning on these trains and we have to sit here far too hot.'

Oblongs of sunlight fall onto Colette's hands. She holds them out in front of her, noticing her own wedding rings on her left finger and her mother's on her right.

Rose says, 'Or far too cold. That's the other thing. Too hot or too cold on these trains.'

'What are you talking about?' says Colette.

'The windows. Where do you drift off to all the time?'

Colette smiles at that. Once, on television, she heard a celebrity say they had a rich inner world which they escaped into whenever they could. That's what Colette thinks she has, too. Nothing matters but what's happening right now and her daydreams. Rose will always be here. Colette says, 'Rose, I'm putting my foot down. We are walking from Blackfriars.'

Rose looks at her and scowls. Then she says, 'Okay, okay. We'll walk.'

The Handover

The five of them were in a dim sum teahouse in Soho. There were tiny lights like diamonds in the walls. A patisserie counter displayed cakes with coconut curls, berries and chocolate shavings. Staff wore black and carried silver trays. They were friends from university and although they didn't all live in London anymore, they tried to see each other as often as possible. One of the women loved two men and neither was her husband. Another was a small, quiet handkerchief of a person, nervous of everything. One treated her daughters to head massages when they behaved. The fourth was a lawyer and had recently painted her bedroom white. Still, every morning her anxiety punched her chest when she woke. There was not much to say about Gina except she was the one they talked about when she wasn't around.

Tea was ordered and arrived in pale ceramic pots. Everyone admired them. Two handsome waiters presented the pastries and cakes. Delighted, the women thanked them and began to explore their desserts with forks. They talked about school uniforms and loft conversions, books they'd read and films they'd seen. Everyone had energetic children and partners with annoying habits, except Gina, but she offered comments that suggested she was interested in their lives.

'I might get another one,' Gina said, as soon as the plates were empty. 'I can't stop thinking about the passion fruit cheesecake. Anyone else?'

'Always so decisive,' said one of the women to Gina. 'How can you be so sure what you want? I'm forever worried I'll make the wrong choice.'

'That sounds familiar,' said someone else. 'I feel rushed off my feet all the time. It's hard to think straight.'

Another had a tip. 'I've given away loads of clothes, loads of the kids' clothes too. Our wardrobes are half empty. There is so much space between every item now.'

Someone said, 'Does it spark joy?'

'No,' she replied. 'But I do save a few minutes in the morning deciding what to wear.' She touched the two women closest to her. 'So good to say that out loud. You can only be yourself with old pals, can't you?'

Gina called to the waiter, tucking a strand of hair behind her ear as she described the cake she wanted. The women glanced at each other.

Someone said, 'Gina, do you never have bad days?'

Gina was fiddling with her watch, looping and unlooping the strap. 'Nope,' she said, sighing. 'You have to learn to let things go.'

A few months later, they went to a play. Gina couldn't join them, so they spent the interval discussing who had seen her recently and who had not, and judging each other based on this knowledge. *They* were the ones with babies and children and puppies to walk. *They* were so busy, as they told each other again and again. What was Gina doing all the time? She didn't post much on Facebook except occasionally a petition or to promote a theatre piece she'd produced. Was she there, though? Looking at their pages and browsing without commenting? They believed she was. Gina rarely replied to them in the WhatsApp group, but they saw she'd read the message. With Gina, what they had was not exactly a friendship, but friendship was what they said it was.

Then it was summer, and the tall buildings flickered in the heat. Children splashed in the fountains by the Queen Elizabeth Hall. A busker's saxophone floated in and out of their conversation as the women sat together on the terrace. That day, Gina had an announcement. She was ending it. The friendship.

She said, 'Don't worry, though. I've found my replacement.'

A woman with blond hair that shone like a mirror lit with sunshine stepped towards them. 'I'm Rachel,' she said, holding out her hand. 'Lovely to meet you.'

They liked her straight away. Rachel had friends in common with someone, and children at the same school as another. She was a project manager and had learned to sew her own vintage dresses. They all said it was really no problem to add an extra chair to the table. After a while, the women caught themselves and realised they had a lot of questions for Gina.

'Are you okay?'

'What happened?'

'I've been offered an amazing opportunity,' Gina told them.

She would be the head programmer for an eco-cruise ship specialising in arts and culture. Instead of tribute bands and comedians, there would be author debates and contemporary dance. The company ran projects engaging port communities. Gina would have a great salary, a spacious cabin and the opportunity to explore the Mediterranean's clear blue waters. She would be in a new phase of life and she would not be keeping in touch.

Rachel said it sounded fantastic. The others quickly agreed.

'I didn't know jobs like that existed.' The woman who said this stared at the steadily rotating London Eye. Then she turned her head sharply. 'Will you have phone reception?'

Gina said no.

'But you could pick up emails?'

'Absolutely not.' Her attention slipped to the skin on her arms.

One said, 'I hope it works out for you. I guess you had to do something, didn't you?'

'What does that mean?' asked Gina, looking up.

'You had so much spare time to fill. All those days. When I'm driving a carload of kids to football early on Saturday mornings, or while planning the week's meals, I'll think of you!'

Gina folded her arms, then let them hang at her sides.

They agreed on a handover period and so met one afternoon at Rachel's house. Her lounge had so many bookcases and there was a brass door handle in the shape of an alligator.

Gina let everyone chat and share news. Then she said to Rachel, 'It's time.'

Rachel held up a bottle of prosecco and gestured for everyone to gather.

One woman stayed near the fireplace. 'I'm not ready. I'm really not ready to say goodbye.'

Gina sighed. 'Here are the memories.' She'd made photobooks, which she passed around. The cover image showed the group standing by ruins in Greece after their final exams. 'What I've done,' she said, 'is select some from each year. I've left space by the photos for your own captions, and spare pages at the back for other pictures.'

'We'll miss you,' said one quiet voice.

'Remember the good times,' said Rachel. She held up the bottle and asked if anyone wanted a top-up. They all did.

The final time they saw each other was at a karaoke bar, which was Rachel's idea. She was always coming up with things like that.

Someone chose 'Son of a Preacher Man', and then cried, because they loved that song. Gina entertained them with Aretha Franklin's 'Respect'. She had her feet planted on the ground, and looked at them all when she sang. When it was time to leave, they asked what they'd done. They wrapped themselves in their coats, wondering if it was more than the job enticing her away. Gina hugged them individually and whispered a different answer to each of them.

Months later, the group met at a Viennese cafe with neat white tablecloths. They sat in green leather chairs. This time the woman who was a lawyer had an announcement. She'd not been sleeping since Gina left. She was distressed. Who would leave the group next?

'We have to be honest with each other,' said someone. 'If there's a problem, just say something.'

'Absolutely,' said Rachel, buttering her toast. She always agreed with everyone and acted as if she knew things they didn't. They had started to find her annoying.

'We can't risk it happening again,' said the lawyer. 'I've had this drawn up.' She showed a contract and explained that she wanted them to sign so no one else abandoned the group.

They each had a copy and flipped through the pages. A few asked questions.

'I'm really not sure,' someone said after a while.

'Me either,' said Rachel.

Someone rolled her eyes. They talked through the terms. They drank coffee and picked at poppy seed scones. The atmosphere was knotty.

'Maybe we all need a break from each other for a while,' said someone.

There was silence, and then they all spoke at once. They couldn't believe it. Two of them went to the bathroom and spent a long time in there, discussing and making an alliance that neither was sure they could keep. When they were back at the table, one asked the others if they knew why Gina left. If there's anything they could have done differently. They eyed each other, making lists in their heads, remembering incidents.

Someone came up with a plan. For their next gathering, each should bring a potential replacement. They would introduce the other women to everyone, and at the end of the evening the core group would vote on who would stay and form the new group.

'It's the only way,' said someone.

'Absolutely,' said Rachel, smiling.

Some Women
Carry Silence
in their Pockets

I awake with a sneeze, which sounds insignificant, but I am the kind of person who sneezes tremendously. The experience is like a thousand tennis balls pummelling every part of my body.

That morning, lying curled in my bed with a heart desperately pumping, I lift my hand to rest on my opposite shoulder and let it stroke me to a calmer place. Scorching sunlight falls from the window, which is the worst thing about renting rooms in an attic with no curtains, but also sometimes the best thing because sweating makes you feel alive. Today I have to drive a long way to sit on a picnic blanket with my dad and his new friends, and to pretend, as ever, I'm an old pal rather than his daughter. I sneeze again and this time follow it with a groan. I roll onto my back, exhausted.

'Bless you!' says a voice. It's my mother.

My eyes zip around the room. 'Are you joking?' I say.

'Over here.' Waving from the pocket of my dressing gown on the back of the door, is my mother. She's leaning on the pocket rim and she's the size of a mouse. 'How's you?'

I'm on my feet, glad for my pyjamas and trying to remember when I last heard her voice. There are so many questions in my mind and the one I find myself asking is, 'Anyone else in there with you?'

'Sorry, no.'

It's a nice dressing gown. Satin with a lace trim. Soft to the touch. The kind of nightwear that slides from your body to floor. A gift from Katie before she met someone else and our relationship splattered on the ground sticky and gross like an egg. 'Okay,' I say.

'It would be better if there were others, too, wouldn't it?' She looks pale and uncertain. 'Is that what you're thinking, Nora?'

We've become the versions of ourselves we only are with each other.

I say, 'I only asked for something to ask.'

My mother grew up as one of seven children. The older four were close, the younger boys were twins. Her fierce father was chairman in the synagogue. He ridiculed them for any show of weakness, saying, 'You were given a mouth wider and bigger than your eyes and ears put together, why don't you use it?' Throughout her life, my mother felt in the way. Even when she definitely should be somewhere; for example, at the birth of her child. 'I'll leave you two to it, shall I?' she famously said, passing my tiny sleeping self over to my dad and the midwife.

My mother sighs. 'I'm sorry. I can go if you like?'

I say, 'It's fine.'

'Are you sure?'

'I said it's fine.'

Needing to think, I start to make my bed and pull at the bottom sheet. My mother. I have thought of her every day since she died. I look around the room, trying to

Gemma Seltzer

imagine what she might think of the place. Where I live has furniture handcrafted from driftwood and organic cotton bedding. An empty desk. The bin is filled with nail varnish bottles after I decided late in the evening that they were pointless additions to my life. I smooth down the duvet and blanket and turn to my mother. 'So, you're in my dressing gown pocket?'

She nods.

'I brought a couple of books, so I wouldn't disturb you too much. When I read, I'll turn the pages quietly.' My mother holds up the tiny volumes.

I crouch in front of her pocket. The writing is small, but I can see one of the titles: *We Should All Be Feminists*.

'Good choice,' I say. All her features have shrunk: the birthmark on her cheek, the wispy strands of hair. I'm ready to ask her about her life now. 'Mum,' I say. A door thumps shut in the house below, then there's a clatter and a dog begins to yap. My head hurts from an evening drinking wine and, the memory now arises, heckling a comedian whose impression of a woman seducing a salad I did not enjoy.

'Bang, crash, wallop,' says my mother, hands pressed to her ears but smiling, too.

'It's Stanley, the spaniel,' I laugh.

I like the dog. We're friends and he often butts his nose on my legs. This is the home of two psychologists called Lydia and Bill, plus their three pre-teen children who speak like adults. The house is enormous, although I don't mind hearing muffled voices or bodies moving around. I find it reassuring. My mother and I talk for a few minutes, before I check my watch and start to think about the food for the picnic I need to buy or make or steal from the fridge downstairs. My mother's mouth is pressed flat so I can't tell if she is happy or in pain.

'Let's have coffee,' I say.

In my kitchen I fill the coffee kettle with water and drop a paper filter onto the ceramic dripper. I spoon out the coffee. This equipment is a gift from the family, and they give me proper ground coffee too. Soon, the air smells of milk chocolate and toffee. I turn on the radio and hear Nigella Lawson's voice. I text my dad: *Your girlfriend is telling* Woman's Hour *listeners how to make fish pie.* Three emojis with hearts for eyes appear on my phone screen in reply. He'll be busy preparing for his celebrations, combing his hair carefully to cover the thin patches.

'You're not going to any trouble, are you?' My mother is nearby, standing on the lino, slightly out of breath. 'You'd tell me if you weren't planning to make coffee? You'd say if you were making it just for me?'

'I really don't mind.' I really don't. At that moment, all kinds of sensations race through my body, including guilt and confusion and love.

From the kitchen window, I watch the houses opposite. There are no other people staring out, just empty rooms bathed in soft pools of light. If this were a fairy tale, I'd have a thimble to hold my mother's drink, or fashion a cup from, say, a leaf. Opening cupboards and drawers, I discover a letter from the Student Loan Company. The paper is stained. Were they my tears? I can't be sure. Eventually, I find a tiny gold Lego trophy in a jar of random things. I drip in the coffee from a spoon. I carry the drinks to the bedroom, my mother following behind me.

'This is best enjoyed black, Mum,' I say, depositing her back into the dressing gown pocket.

Gemma Seltzer

'Delicious,' my mother says before she takes a sip. 'Do you mind if I ask you something? Just say if you'd mind.'

'Okay.'

'You'd say if you minded, wouldn't you?'

She really is the same as ever. I say, 'Yeah.'

'Are you sure?' She has lowered her eyes.

'Just ask me!'

My mother takes a breath. 'Would it be possible for you to call me Venetia?'

'Venetia?' I burst out laughing. I wrap my hands around my hot mug.

'I always wanted to be called Venetia.' My mother seems comfortable in the dressing gown. It must take a mix of balance and stamina to stand up in the pocket.

'You don't want me to call you by your actual name?'

'I've had the name so long.'

'Or, "Mum"?'

'It's a bit, well, formal, isn't it?'

I study my fingernails and think this set of circumstances makes so much sense for a woman always so afraid to take up space. 'Is it?' I say.

'I'm sorry, do you mind?'

'No.'

'You always were such a good girl.'

Those words from her mouth lick me like a flame. We stare at the walls. What I could now do is ask her to climb into my hands, hold her there and then squash her and squeeze her until she can't breathe. A phone rings down in the house below, so I decide not to continue that line of thinking. Instead, I tell her about the family. How Lydia creates meals based on the latest events in their lives. It's her way of affirming the family ties. So, before a difficult exam, there might be lasagne to represent layers of knowledge melting together to make a perfect dish. For a successful rugby match, they would have potato salad. Oval-shaped. Chicken drumsticks for band practice, and so on.

'I have to join them on Friday nights. They say it's not compulsory, but if I don't they yell my name until I answer. It's hard to say no when their five hopeful faces stare up at you from the bottom of the stairs.'

'Oh, Jewish?'

'Yup.' I don't offer any opinions on this.

'That's nice,' she says. 'I always hoped you'd have some Jewish things in your life. And I thought they looked nice when I walked in the front door.'

My mind rushes to absorb this information. How her little hand might have knocked on the wood, or how she slipped in when the door was open for the postman, and how she climbed the stairs – all the stairs! – or maybe she leaped onto Stanley's furry back, slapped his side, and dashed up to my room, screaming and barking. Now I know how she got here, should I ask how she found me? And, how long she is staying. And then, what happens to a person's soul after they die.

'Are you hungry?' I ask. I head to the kitchen to make some toast with honey on top. It's fun to cut food into tiny squares for your mother.

We eat our breakfast in our corners of the room and I tell her about my job. I transcribe film and audio recordings. My tasks appear in a list when I log onto the system. 'They call me the fastest typist in the west,' I say, with pride.

My mother nods. 'Wonderful,' she says.

I wait, knowing I want more, knowing I won't get it. It's familiar, this feeling.

The company I work for has developed audio transcription software, which picks up errors and is worth a lot of money. I'm a professional transcriptionist, overseeing the conversion to text. 'I'm really well paid,' I say. 'I like it a lot.'

Not entirely true. Katie was the first person I wanted to tell the stories I had sealed in boxes in my mind. She had good scissors and helped me open them. Now she's gone, I have a life that includes days when I don't speak to anyone at all. The job involves sitting alone at home or in coffee shops with noise-cancelling headphones.

'Congratulations,' my mother says.

'Thanks,' I reply. 'Venetia.'

She clasps her tiny hands together in the pocket, so pleased.

We're on our way to the supermarket. I know I should buy birthday cake, or something, for today. I also know that the definition of a competent human being is someone who spends their money well in Budgens and understands all the special offers. As we walk, my mother moves around in my pocket, similar to a hamster burrowing. She's humming quietly, and then so am I. We talk and point things out to each other. There are half a dozen other women on the pavements. We see them all, some with Nordic walking poles, some with efficient hairstyles, others with buggies containing toddlers poking crackers and carrot sticks into their mouths. Aside from the drama of parakeets screeching overhead, Belsize Park is harmonious.

'The natural world is a marvel,' my mother says, settling back against my body.

'Hey, Mum? Venetia?' I look down at her face. 'I have a question.'

'Okay, of course. I'll try my best to answer.'

I pause before I speak, leaving her dangling and enjoying it. 'When did my hands start to look like this?' I flex them back and forth. 'The skin is looser than it used to be, there are wrinkles, my thumbs look bloated.' What she can't say is that she doesn't know. That she missed a lot of my youth because she was in a haze and my twenties because she wasn't around. 'When did it happen, Mum?' I ask again when we're in the supermarket car park.

She waits a moment. 'I don't know. You think too much.'

I show her my hands again, pulling at the loose skin, running a finger along the knuckles. 'This isn't thinking, it's seeing.'

'Well, you see too much.'

I tuck my hand in the pocket. She reaches out and places her palm on one of my fingers. It's the size of a staple, and I barely feel its weight, but it's significant.

'Do you think he'll remember me?' whispers my mum, sitting on the edge of my desk and swinging her legs. She is asking about my dad and his life. After she died, we stayed in the same South London home, but a year ago he packed everything into boxes and found a place by the sea in Hove.

Gemma Seltzer

He found his kind: vague but passionate vegans, eager but inattentive hill walkers. They were forever having accidents on their hikes. Every time we spoke, someone had broken, sprained or damaged a body part.

'I'd rather not get involved,' I say, moving around the room and looking for spare jumpers and socks. 'It's between the two of you.' I keep holding things in my hand, then discarding them, unsure what I need. Clothes with pockets, for sure.

My mother and I eventually leave at lunchtime. In the car, I heap shopping bags and extra items like a rug and a kite and half my wardrobe. We take some time deciding on how best to arrange ourselves and eventually work out she feels safest tucked in my jacket pocket.

'Moving vehicles make me nervous,' she says.

I describe things I can see from the windscreen: a robin in the bushes, where the fence had been fixed at the playground. A few huge lorries lumber by. With Paul Simon playing in the car, I can face anything.

The journey turns into a serious motorway, accompanied by industrial estates, warehouses and tower blocks high in the sky. Up there, no one would see you wave, I think.

'You'll let me know when we're out of the city, won't you?' my mother asks. 'I want to see all the trees.'

A truck driver throws a crisp packet from his window. Caught in the wind, it flies high for a while then is lost under a set of car wheels. As we drive, I find I'm thinking about how cruel I could be to my tiny mother. I could not tell her when we leave London. Not even talk to her again. She'd sit in my pocket and I'd say nothing. I shake my head and remember how my mother used to pretend she was invisible. On her sewing machine, she often made shirts or dresses from the same patterned fabric as her cushions or tablecloths. On the sofa, wearing her new clothes, she'd laugh, shifting positions and asking us over and over if we could see her. She loved it when we said we couldn't.

After a while, the road dips and we scream as if we're on a fairground ride. We rise up again by hedgerows and fields. The sun peeks through the treetops and I lift my mother onto the dashboard. She arranges herself in an empty compartment as I drive along country lanes. We park in a place surrounded by wild spindly grass, swaying in the wind. My mother is keen to be outside. She crouches under the car to relieve herself.

'Just in time to save me from an embarrassing accident,' she says, adjusting her belt when she reappears. 'I would do anything for you not to have to worry about me.'

We follow a pathway upwards. It leads to a view of green hills, slow-moving sheep and distant rooftops. I recognise a group of people with sun hats, carrier bags and picnic baskets. One woman runs her fingers along a hedge. Ten or eleven other adults in wafts of clothes, pastel capes and abundant scarves, chatter and bounce along. We walk towards them and my mother's head peeks from my pocket.

'Greetings,' I say to a few people. I crouch to help unpack blankets and lay out plates of food. Someone notifies the group that everything is vegetarian. I discreetly add my bourbon biscuits and Mr Kipling apple pies to a pile of packets. Then my dad calls my name. I stand up and he is pretending he is a pirate, spying me through his invisible telescope.

'Happy birthday to me!' he says, arm over my shoulder and walking me a few steps from the group. When he turns to me, I notice his T-shirt has GUACAMOLE printed on the front. 'Hello, Nora!'

'Of all the places to see you!' I say.

Everything we say is cheerful. We remember the last time we saw each other: at his brother's fancy-dress party when he wore a gorilla costume, though he could have arrived bare-chested and got away with it! We move on to talk about how expensive things are. For example, petrol, beer and houses.

My dad says, 'I'm going to stay forever in Hove. We don't believe in money here.'

Is he going to annoy me already? 'Wait, you don't think money exists?' I shove my hands into my pockets without thinking, but quickly remove them when I hear a squeak.

'And how are you?' asks my dad.

I fold my arms over my chest. 'Great!'

'Great?'

'Excellent.' He's obviously the last person I'd tell about my emotional state and about the arrival of my tiny mother.

'How's Katie?'

I tighten my grip on myself. 'Gone.'

My dad is suddenly asking lots of questions, wondering why I hadn't told him. Didn't I know I could call him anytime? Over by the blankets, I see a man help a woman open the lid of a Tupperware box, touching her on the waist as he leans in. My eyes fill with tears. It's ridiculous, I know, but I feel I am waiting for something and I am afraid it will not come.

I listen to my dad say something about how society is a machine and we are all prisoners, anyway. He's read a book on the subject and he recommends it to me. We wander back to the group and my dad elbows me, aiming for affection and my arm but instead jabbing at my chest. It's awkward, but we both ignore it.

'This is Nora,' my dad says, leaning towards the woman who loved the hedge. She has on a baseball cap that leaves most of her face in the shade. She doesn't seem able to look me in my eyes, only nearby, like my ear or my chin. 'If she was a Beatles song,' says my dad, 'she'd be "Lucy in the Sky with Diamonds". What would yours be?' Then leaves us to it, satisfied with his introductions.

My mother pokes her head out from the pocket. 'I'm "Ob-La-Di, Ob-La-Da" but I know that's a silly song.'

The woman doesn't hear her, she's talking about George Harrison's eating habits.

'I wish I hadn't said anything,' whispers my mother.

I keep smiling at the woman, who is staring at my shoulder. At the same time, I'm pushing the person in my pocket back down. After a few minutes, I learn that the woman is a 'Love Me Do' sort of person, and we both know that means we won't get along. I excuse myself and find a spot on the picnic blanket to begin a forceful conversation with someone about the comedian's salad sketch. It's of no interest to them, but I keep repeating the bad punchlines.

More people start to arrive. They slap my dad on the back, offering him wrapped boxes and enveloped cards. No one really talks to me, and I don't bother with them either. My dad pops over periodically, then darts back to welcome new people. Later in the afternoon, we sing happy birthday and I eat three different kinds of cake.

Gemma Seltzer

My mother has crept out of my pocket, and sits by my side, surveying the picnic scene. 'I don't think these people are your father's real friends,' she says. 'I didn't want to say anything and I'm probably wrong.'

I look at my feet stuffed into my trainers. Turning them on the side I wonder whether I will ever be the kind of woman to wear heels.

When I was eight years old, while my dad was working away, my mother asked if we could swap rooms. I didn't need convincing. I was in my nightdress with two teddies tucked under my arm, so I leaped into her big double bed, gathered the lovely silky pillows and creamy covers around myself as if they were clouds, and fell asleep.

Meanwhile, she pulled the *My Little Pony* duvet over her body and sank into the mattress. When my dad returned the next evening, he was not impressed that I had eaten crisps all day, yet saved most of his concern for my mother's health.

'We have a problem,' I heard him say into the telephone. 'She's got lost again.'

That evening, we watched her sleeping body vibrate with painful snores that tore at her throat. The sour smell of her breath made me gag, but my dad gripped my fingers when I tried to pull away. I remember how car headlights flashed into the room through a gap in the curtains. On the bedside table there were loads of discarded tissues squeezed into balls. My mother's eyelids quivered, and her mouth hung open.

I jiggled my fingers on the lump, my mother. 'Mum! Let's go!'

'Nora,' said my dad, softly.

There was no reply. No movement.

'Mum!'

I started to bang my fists on her body, over and along all the *My Little Pony* figures with their too-large eyes and colourful bodies.

'It's not fair!' I started to cry.

'Please, just ignore me,' she said in a tiny voice. 'I'm sorry.'

My mother stayed in my bed for twenty-nine days. Appointments were made: the doctor, the clinic, the rabbi, the therapist, flower arranging, walking groups, but she never attended. We brought her sandwiches or soup or stew on a tray with a newspaper and a serviette, and she ate hidden under the covers. One day, though, she got up. She had a bath, invited friends over for lunch, sewed a new dress, and life went back to normal. This was the pattern for years. Brightness, then hiding from the world again. Brightness, then bed. We lost her for good when I was nineteen. Brightness, bed, then gone.

At the picnic, I drink Diet Coke. The fizz cheers me up. One of my dad's friends has an actual 1980s Walkman and serenades us with whale sounds from a cassette. I hear my mother call my name. And then I'm laughing because I see she is stumbling across the picnic blanket. I watch her disappear into a hole in the fabric, then pop up again, thrusting her head and shoulders through the gap. She's like a cake doll, with the fabric rising around her. My

Gemma Seltzer

mother's skirt is not made of sponge and icing, but has a red tartan pattern.

'Look at my dress!' she calls, swaying and grinning.

I realise no one else has noticed the tiny woman whose head is poking through the blanket. They don't seem to see her hands, or shoulders, or her face with its sweet little nose, ears and mouth.

'It's silly, I know. I shouldn't be doing this, should I?' She is laughing so hard.

'Venetia, you're amazing,' I say.

I should try to rationalise all this. Or tell my dad that the weirdest thing has happened, but I won't. At least not for a while, not on his birthday. Instead, I watch my mother look delightedly around at me and at everything: the people having ordinary days eating crisps, while drones buzz in the sky and crows dig for treasure in rubbish bins.

Get Away from Earth Awhile

Andie unbuttons her dress and lets it fall away. She kicks off her sandals, picks up her cardigan, and runs towards a solid, ancient-looking oak tree. Her chin points towards the top and up, up, up she goes, fingers tight to trunk, bark scraping skin. Andie is dressed in only her underwear. She settles on a branch, closes her eyes, and strokes the cardigan as though it is a sleeping animal. A small crowd forms under the tree. Andie's phone rings its distinctive sound: a recording of her friend Leah coughing. Everyone has a different story for why there is a woman in a tree and none of them are right.

The sun reached its highest point and the air was thick with heat. People moved slowly, stumbling along the train platform at Gipsy Hill. They were too hot. Their soft, bare arms bashed into each other as they aimed towards the ticket hall. A woman's voice on a loudspeaker told people they should carry water at all times, and not board a train if they felt unwell. What if reaching your destination is the thing that makes you sick? Andie thought.

Outside, she crossed a road and followed the crowd up the hill. They passed a petrol station forecourt and the

Golden Fry chip shop. The transmitter tower's slender lattice frame rose in a sky empty of clouds. Gradually the mass eased as people slipped into side roads. Further on were nice painted houses, but all had front gardens with shrivelled hedges and wilting flowers. Sweat and white deodorant stains marked Andie's dress. Cars drove by. Approaching the church, Andie noted the large cross hung on the building. A group of women in floral dresses stood chattering outside. On the pavement opposite, Andie paused and waited for the nausea to pass. This was weather that scared you, burned skin, skewed everything. The ceremony was in forty-five minutes.

'Can I help, dear?' said a man sitting in the shade of a bus stop. He was wearing a bowtie and waved his newspaper with the headline: *Heatwave!* Today was the highest summer temperature on record. He called, 'What are you looking for?'

Andie stared at the church and threw over a reply. 'Jesus. I'm looking for Jesus.'

He laughed. 'You're in the right place, my friend. If you seek him, he will be found.'

'Wish he'd hurry up,' said Andie. She had an image in her mind of Jesus arriving on a horse. Probably not a white one, because Jesus wasn't cheesy, but chestnut-coloured with flowing hair. He'd canter up the hill and when he reached her, Jesus would say, 'Howdy!' The real question was whether she would linger outside the church for Jesus, or not. Sweat gathered behind her knees and along her back. 'Is Jesus coming today, do you think?'

'Could be,' said the man. He noticed a bus lumbering towards them and stood. 'Could be this very Sunday.'

The hot pavement burned through Andie's sandals. She said, 'I think I need something more definite.' She waved farewell.

Further up the hill was the hub of Crystal Palace. Busy women held shopping bags. Lycra cyclists wheeled bikes. New parents rocked prams and talked while sipping coffee in reusable cups. Andie walked through, raising her elbows like chicken wings to allow a breeze under her arms and to budge people out of her way.

Andie's tree doesn't have lots of leaves. Although she often likes to pretend things that are not true are in fact true, she has to admit that she's fairly visible in the tree. She had paused at one of the first sturdy limbs, swinging a foot over to straddle it. She views the lake and swings her legs back and forth. A lumpy stone dinosaur mounts a tree stump. Moorhens paddle.

It is cooler up in the tree. Andie relaxes her head against the trunk. Time then divides into the moments when she shrugs off her cardigan and lays it on her lap, and those when she slots her arms back into the sleeves. She wobbles on the branch to balance. During the first kind of moment, the air warms her skin and the sun shines through the leaves onto her shoulders. Sunlit, her knickers are elegant, and it seems appropriate to show the world her pretty lace bra. Andie thinks she might live a happier life if she stays in the tree. She will not lose hours trying to have unique experiences in London, or writing manifestos to live by. But it would be hard to charge her laptop and answer emails from here. With cardigan off, children shout their own cute names, and jump in dust, delighted.

Clouds cover the sun. Andie's skin goosebumps and a group of men appear below with beer cans. They lob their dog into the lake. 'What kind of people!' she shouts, putting on her cardigan. A jogger slows down, and looks directly at her, then continues on.

This trip to Crystal Palace must not be pointless. Something more interesting than Leah's summer wedding must happen. A church wedding with sweet peas on each pew and dramatic windows letting in all the world's light. Andie is thirsty now; her mouth is dry. Something else has to happen today, or else she will simply be someone who went to her friend's wedding. She sprayed sun lotion all over her body this morning! Her minimum hope for the day is a tan. So, she unbuttons the cardigan and drops it to the ground.

The evening before, Andie had reviewed the TfL website. She'd studied a blog suspicious of the high number of lost dog notices in Crystal Palace. Was there a canine thief lurking in the area, the article wondered? Around one in the morning, she located the wedding invite. She purchased a jolly Cath Kidston oven glove from the online gift registry. Deciding to go, she was firm in her mind about why. Because she was probably a good friend. Then again, who could she ask to check? Her ridiculous parents had booked themselves on a three-month cruise. Most of her friends lived in modern towns outside London or villages with limited phone signal. 'I can't hear you!' they shouted into handsets. 'You're cutting

out!' People got old and felt city life had cheated them. They'd been sprinting for so many years and never won the race, and now spent their days waving mobiles above their heads. Andie was always trying not to take it personally.

'Are those from Marks and Spencer?' calls a woman wearing a red-striped dress that reaches the floor. 'I think I have a similar set.'

'What's from Marks and Spencer?' An older woman, also in a long dress, but navy blue, says. She's similar enough in face and gesture to suggest she is the other's mother. 'What from where?'

'Her bra and pants,' says the younger woman, pointing to Andie.

'No, I don't think so, Heather. Look too expensive.'

Andie smiles at that. She feels warm and alluring.

The mother squints and says, 'Why are you up there?'

Andie shrugs.

'Well, will you please come down?'

Andie considers this, because the question was asked so politely. Then, she is distracted by how the woman scrunched her face.

'No, I won't,' says Andie.

'You dropped something.' Heather gestures towards the cardigan.

Andie frowns. Staring down, she wonders how to respond. 'It isn't mine,' she says. 'Or that dress over there. They're not mine.'

Both women tilt their heads to look.

Heather says, 'Fine. We just wanted to sit here to read an article together.'

'Be my guests,' says Andie. 'I don't own the tree.'

'I suppose not. Okay then.'

'Have a wonderful time.'

The two women sit, arranging their clothes and legs. With a magazine between them, they begin to study the first page. Moments pass but they can't settle. 'Are you okay? Do you need anything?' calls the older woman.

'Leave her alone, Mum.'

The mother can't stop trying to help. 'I could get you an ice cream from the van,' she says. 'There's a van over there, and I don't mind.'

'Okay,' says Andie.

The mother leaves and Andie watches the fabric of her dress swish as she walks. Heather remains. She stays seated and pecks her finger at a digital watch to check something vital. Beep beep beep.

Andie's company held a party recently. From the office window, the Shard poked upwards into the sky. Pumping up balloons in the corner were three clowns, each with a straw hat and red nose, but not painted faces. These were modern clowns: clowns by vocation. Andie's afternoon job involved identifying, interviewing and recruiting clowns. She designed an exercise: candidates had to create a ten-minute routine for someone afraid of the letter P. It was a good test, she thought, if they could entertain in difficult circumstances, they could certainly manage the hospices and the children's wards.

A man had made an effort to speak to her, even though she positioned herself behind the rows of stacked chairs studying her quiz sheet. What *was* the capital of Brazil? He picked his way to her corner, greeting her with a deep bow. Dom, his name was, and he worked in the corporate fundraising team. Wore a tiny top hat. Smelled like a bathroom.

'Do you like to dance?' Dom had asked.

It had been a successful year for clowns in hospitals. The music was loud with an actual DJ playing records. Around the room, groups of people in spotty or colourful clothes stood chatting and swaying to the songs.

Although she was always dancing in her tiny kitchen, to Dom, Andie said, 'I don't.'

But then the song shifted from 'All the Single Ladies' to '9 to 5'. He held out his hand and she found she took it in her own. She and Dom danced. After Dolly came 'Summer Holiday' and then 'Wouldn't it be Nice'. They laughed and talked. She remembered everything. Later, at home, she'd pressed her own hand to the curve of her back. She skipped around in her living room with a feather boa gifted from a retiring clown. Monday came and went, as did the entire week, and she did not see Dom. She eventually asked someone and heard the party had been Dom's last day at the charity. So, that was that.

Andie breathes in the smell of sweet leaves. She calls down, 'So, what are you reading?'

'An article,' the young woman, Heather, replies without looking up.

'Right.'

People in the park wander by wearing vest tops and denim shorts. Her cardigan lies abandoned like a sleeping princess awaiting some guy's kiss. Andie had bought it from a shop beyond her lifestyle. A minimalist boutique without hangers. Garments were draped on a variety of chaise longues. She'd ducked into the shop to avoid a girl from school who was wearing head to toe denim. Inside, she scooped up a cardigan, dashed into the changing room and pulled the curtain shut. The cardigan was fancy, with half sleeves that billowed and sparkly embroidered detail on the cuffs. In the changing room, it looked friendly as a bird, happy as a garden rose, but it failed in real life.

When Andie got the phone call, she was waiting outside the British Museum for her tour group to arrive. Every weekday morning during the summer she wore a bright orange cap and ticked names off a list. The clipboard was also orange, and so were the wristbands she gave to each person. Today it was Spanish kids. The girls would have braces and laugh behind their hands. The boys would be practising their new voices. Andie would guide them through the collections, stopping at the Rosetta Stone and the Egyptian mummies, revealing the stories she'd recited for years. She didn't even have to communicate directly, as the teachers took turns to translate and repeat questions. Andie barely paid attention.

The phone call was from Leah, who said, 'Guess what? You'll never guess! Solomon asked me to marry him and I said yes. Of course, I said yes!'

Andie squealed first of all, because Leah was her oldest friend. She saw the scene already: small nieces as bridesmaids, reading the entwined tree roots quote from *Captain Corelli's Mandolin*, mothers wandering around drunk on champagne and pride. Then another feeling rose. Disappointment. A train had stopped and Leah had got on it, and was now chugging off into the distance. No one else they knew was married, because they agreed weddings were lame. They always said they wouldn't support an outdated institution created by men for men to retain economic power and authority over women. Writing your own vows didn't change that. Leah had shaved hair, opinions and suspicious eyes. She'd had H-A-T-E tattooed on her knuckles.

Andie suddenly realised what was happening. She laughed. In the distance she saw a coach turn the corner. This was probably her group. 'Very funny. I believed you. What are you really calling for?'

'Seriously,' said Leah. 'Save the date. Nineteenth of June. I'm going to have the whole church thing, and a choir, and wear white.'

'Leah!' Andie was struggling. At university, Leah smoked, scathed, startled. In lectures, she would cough up phlegm from her throat, swill it in her mouth and hurl it into the hair of any girl in front. Andie never had phlegm in her hair, and for that she was always grateful. 'With a vicar?'

'Yes! His name is Fred. It's going to be very cool. Instead of walking down the aisle, I'll be on a skateboard.'

'You're joking.'

'I'm not. Andie. Why are you being weird?'

'It's marriage, Leah.'

'Don't be bitter.'

'Don't be a facsimile of every other woman who ever existed. I thought you had principles.' Andie regretted the words as soon as she said them.

Leah paused. 'Solomon and I are reclaiming the traditions and making them our own.'

The coach stopped and young people poured down from the steps, laughing as they were released into the day. Andie saw a batch of them block the pavement, marvelling at something on a phone.

Andie said, 'I have to go.' She waved her clipboard to the group and directed them towards the museum gates.

Leah and Andie didn't really talk after that. Only a few text messages and a note to let her know she was invited to the hen party. The first email about that asked them all to contribute eight photos, a favourite song, a significant memory, a lock of hair, and a hundred pounds to a central kitty. Andie didn't bother replying.

In the tree in Crystal Palace Park, Andie shifts position. A breeze touches her skin. She hears her phone ring again: cough, cough, cough. The park has woodland areas, open grassland with brave people in swimwear, stretched out on towels and boiling under the heat.

The mother returns. They now have to solve the problem of how to pass the ice cream to Andie.

'Throw it please. I'll catch.' Andie smiles. The day is ~ning out to be unexpectedly enjoyable.

~he older woman is alarmed. 'What if you fall?'

'We have to try,' says Andie. She adjusts her bra straps and holds out her hands.

'Would you prefer a Magnum, Solero or a lemonade lolly?'

'Magnum,' say Andie and Heather at the same time.

'Oh dear,' says the mother.

'Don't worry, I never get anything I want,' says Andie. An old trick, but if they feel sorry for her, she'll get the right ice cream.

The young woman has her own plan. 'The lolly is more robust. It could stand being dropped. The others, I'm not sure. Throw the lolly up, see if she catches it.'

'Okay,' says the mother but doesn't move.

'Give it to me.' The daughter grabs the lolly and tosses it at Andie.

It might have hit her shoulder if Andie hadn't swung to the left. 'Careful!'

They all watch the packet drop to the ground with a thud. A moorhen flaps in the water in response. There is a coughing sound nearby, still.

'What is that noise?' says the mother.

Heather says, 'You could have caught that if you'd tried.' Her voice is tight.

'You'd better have that one, darling.'

'Mum!'

They exchange a look which seems to have a deep history, because then the younger woman says, 'Fine.' She goes towards the lolly and picks it up.

The man Leah is marrying is an artist. Solomon paints the walls in their flat and watches them dry, noting down ideas that strike him as he works. It keeps him occupied for days on end. Leah says he has a calming influence and they spend their weekend in hardware shops looking for brushes and rollers. They whisper to each other when they're together. Andie thinks the boredom of his company has anaesthetised Leah. But who is she to judge?

'It's too hot and I'm guest number thirty-nine,' says Andie, rubbing a finger over her branch. That is the actual number listed in pencil on the back of the invitation. Her surname is Asher, which should have placed her in prime position on an alphabetical guest list.

'What does that mean?' says Heather.

'No one understands me,' says Andie.

'Shall I throw the ice cream?' says the older woman.

'Go and give it to her if you're so desperate for her to eat,' says Heather. She sucks aggressively on her lolly.

The woman sighs, and then moves towards the trunk of the tree. She tucks the Magnum and her Solero into her pockets.

'You're not serious!' shouts Heather. She pulls at her mother's arm. 'You'll break something! You're all slippery and sweaty.'

The other woman is marching forward, she has in her mind what she needs to do. 'I'll pull myself along a bit, so I can pass it to her.'

Andie isn't worried. 'Great idea,' she calls down, turning to watch. The branches are inviting, they form a sort of spiral staircase circling the trunk, so it's actually much easier to climb than you might think. A lot of things are much easier to do than other people imagine.

The other woman ties her dress in a knot above her waist.

'Mum!' her daughter calls. 'I can see your pants!'

'Enjoy!'

Steadily, she climbs up and then she is nesting on the fork of a neighbouring branch above the grass, skin covered in sap, scraped palms.

'Welcome,' says Andie.

'Here's your Magnum.' The woman has flushed cheeks and a line of sweat along her hairline.

Andie takes the ice cream and lets the wrapper fall to the ground. The other woman does the same. They lick and talk together for some time.

'What are you saying?' calls Heather. 'What are you speaking about?'

They don't answer. A few more people appear below, and Heather turns her attention to them, explaining the situation. One woman scaled a tree, and now another one, her actual mother, is up there, too. They are sat on branches, sheltering from the heat. Andie waves down and smiles. She feels giddy.

Andie fell into a canal once. She was drunk on wine, the music from the warehouse party still vibrating around her body. With Leah and their friends, she had been walking home from Haggerston in the early hours. It was a warm evening, and the high walls along the towpath gave plenty of shadows for people to meet. People danced along shouting and singing. The full moon shone in an immaculate gleaming circle above their heads.

Andie still remembers enjoying the sensation of weightlessness as she tripped and flew into the canal. She heard sound around her, but muted, far away. In the quiet, she was happy. She felt the liquid rush through her nose, down the back of her throat, into her lungs. The pain began in her stomach, where the water hit like a rising punch. Then came a thick arm underneath and she was flying. Leah held her as she barked water. The two of them sat together by the canal, chests heaving, wet bodies touching. Overwhelmed, both Andie and Leah cried. People offered their jackets to wrap around her shoulders. Everyone thought they should put up railings because accidents happen, but Andie was glad for the moment. Before then, she hadn't known Leah cared.

'Are you okay up there, Mum?' Heather is looking up at her mother, with a small amount of admiration in her voice. 'Do you feel safe?'

The older woman says, 'I can see for miles.'

Both she and Andie stare ahead. Dinosaurs line the water's edge with their square features and heavy feet. All around are huge ferns with dried edges, and purple flowers. People stand nearby, watching and waiting.

Andie's body pulses and sweats. 'The dinosaurs are the only things here not dying.' The rattling noise of the leaves seems to answer. She looks down at herself, sees blotchy red

Gemma Seltzer

skin on her chest and feels the press of heavy heat. Things suddenly feel urgent. Where is her phone? 'Oh Jesus. What's the time?' she calls out.

'About three o'clock,' says Heather from down below, checking her watch.

Andie says, 'I'd better go.' Then, she clambers along the branch, which is tricky as she has to squeeze by the other woman, but they manage. Andie drops from the tree. She picks up all her things, and sprints away. 'Thank you! Bye!'

'Are you coming down, Mum?' says Heather, eyeing the crowd. 'Let's go.'

In the distance, there's a repeated thud of a football being kicked. The woman up the tree twists her ankles together and swings her legs.

'No,' she says. 'I think I'll stay awhile.'

Should a Catastrophe Occur

Ruth parks the car then she and her daughters, Sara and Grace, dash through wet streets laughing under a shared umbrella. The rain comes down in sheets, while thunder bellows and a dog barks mightily.

'This weather!' says Sara, the oldest, flicking a sodden leaf from her anorak. 'It's like someone emptying a bucket on our heads.'

'It's because of the fossil fuel industry,' Ruth says, voice raised above the downpour.

Her fourteen-year-old, Grace, is trying to cover the three of them with a single umbrella, while using her spare hand to hold her hood. 'Yeah, yeah.'

The girls are shrieking now. It's new to them, this area of London, which they see as they rush along Streatham High Road. Displays of open-mouthed silver fish – bodies shining on piles of ice, a bakery with a mountain of croissants in the shop window, and the swoosh of a bus sliding through puddles.

'I'm serious!' Ruth can't remember when her fears began to rise about extreme weather, but since they began, they haven't stopped. 'You've seen the documentaries!' Trails of rain run into her ears.

Grace says, 'I just thought, did anyone bring a hairbrush?'

Sara calls her an idiot. Ruth tells them to be nice. The rucksack on her back suddenly feels heavy, her long ponytail caught in the straps. She thinks about the epic tidal storm that will eventually engulf most of the world. The question is when. *God?* she asks. *Is today the day?*

Turning up a steep side street, they spot the synagogue.

'I can't breathe; I need to give up smoking,' says Sara, panting. She slows down, picking her way across broken paving slabs in her wedges.

'What?' Ruth says. Her own mother died of lung cancer only a few years ago.

'Joking!'

Grace sprints up the synagogue steps and knocks on the stately wooden doors. As the other two join her, an entryway nearby opens and a woman wearing a flat cap, trouser suit, and an earpiece beckons them. *A decoy door and trained security staff,* Ruth thinks. *Excellent.*

Inside, Ruth leads them up two flights of stairs to the synagogue sanctuary. They stand at the back, scanning the room. The lighting is warm and welcoming, with lamps glowing by each row of seats. A golden ark stands on a raised platform with doves decorating its doors. Rain thrashes against the windows, causing the frames to rattle, but Ruth feels safe inside. Grace rakes her fingers through her hair, encouraging the others to do the same.

'So much wood,' Sara says as she smooths her stray strands.

Ruth agrees, both palms on her scalp steadily drawn downwards. Useful, should they choose this building as a designated safe place and need to build a fire.

The rabbi pops up by their side. She has fair hair in a bob and beaming eyes, and while she doesn't hug them, she looks like one day she might.

Gemma Seltzer

'Welcome! You must be Ruth.'

'Rabbi Rebecca?' Ruth emailed in advance and knows she should reference their conversation about her renewed interest in Jewish things, but she is distracted by the other woman's sweet dimples, the way her fringe flicks.

'Student Rabbi Rebecca, actually. I'm new to all this!' She looks around astonished, as if she has never been inside a synagogue.

There's a gap, while Ruth searches for words to respond. Her eyes dart over Rabbi Rebecca's forehead, cheeks and chin.

'Right,' says Sara, holding out a hand. 'Well, we are Ruth's lovely daughters, Sara and Grace. Our dad, Ben, recently died.'

Ruth's heart stumbles. She stares at these almost-adults, these women.

'Hullaballoo!' says the rabbi.

'What?' says Ruth.

'So sorry, I tend to say fun things when I haven't quite got the right words. It can lighten the mood. But I'm sorry to hear about your loss. I wish you all a long life.'

The girls smile and say ordinary things. They nod as the different features of the sanctuary are emphasised. Other families enter the room. 'Shabbat shalom,' they all say. Ruth, Sara and Grace file along a pew and take a seat. 'I've got a wet bottom,' says Grace.

'Too much information,' says Sara.

During the service, a man calls page numbers so they can follow the prayers. When someone opens the ark, the girls rise from their seats like pets she has trained. Outside, the storm decides enough is enough. Rain reduces to a patter and Ruth enters her thoughts. They have good evacuation plans, overall. Should a catastrophe occur, Ruth will be in the office, at home, the supermarket or the petrol station. The girls both at school. They'll meet in the disused warehouse beside the railway station where they have a store. The synagogue building may offer an alternative, should roads be blocked or flooded.

After the rabbi's speech, which includes the words 'jabberwocky' and 'buttertrees', Grace leans over to whisper. 'It's time, Mum.'

'Good luck,' says Sara from the corner of her mouth.

Ruth grabs the backpack and makes her way out of the sanctuary. She must cover the basement for which Plan F allocates ten minutes. Sara will follow in ninety seconds to survey the ground floor. They will then meet to return together, as if they've merely been talking in the bathroom or corridor as women do. Focused on her task, Ruth runs down the staircase. In the main hall, people arrange platters and flowers for the kiddush.

An older man with white puffs of hair and a toddler in his arms calls, 'Where's the fire?' Then, 'You don't want to meet my granddaughter?'

'I need the toilet!' Ruth replies.

She pushes open the first door downstairs and finds a gloomy, abandoned room. Behind other doors there are computers and books. Mops and cleaning equipment. Old files and newspapers. One room is a bathroom with six cubicles and six pink sinks. Each stiff, rusty tap is tested, each floor tile checked. Back in the corridor, Ruth sees a cupboard with slatted doors. 'This is the place,' she says to herself and unclips her backpack. From its depths, she takes

Gemma Seltzer

a travel blanket, water purification tablets, soup tins, a can opener, and dried fruit and nut bars sealed in an airtight container. Organising the goods into the cupboard, she pictures a sun rising over a fresh, wide lavender field at the midpoint of summer.

Suddenly, there's a voice. 'Have you found something interesting?'

Ruth pauses and looks around. The man she saw earlier is bouncing the child on his hip. 'This is not in the plan,' she says and climbs into the cupboard, pulling the door shut.

'I didn't hear what you said,' the man says, voice muffled. 'I don't even know your name.' He knocks on the door. 'Mrs No Name? Can I help?'

Ruth doesn't reply. Her eyes take time to adjust to the dark, but soon she makes out her hand in front. She hears the man sigh and talk to his granddaughter. Here in the cupboard, Ruth can finally think about things. For a start, Ben. He listened to piano concertos quietly because he enjoyed challenging himself to hear the softer notes. A man she loved, but who didn't leave much of a footprint on life. Their friends would retell him his own funny anecdotes. If a flood came, Ruth knows her heart wouldn't have been able to cope with protecting their daughters and him, too.

She's perched on the boxes containing the fruit and nut bars. Her skin feels damp still, but not unpleasantly so. This habit of keeping close to you all the things you need is something Ruth's mother would have understood. They lived in a small house in Leyton with sticky linoleum in the hallways, bathroom and kitchen. Her mother who always said Ruth was too thin, and that men liked to grab hold of a woman. 'There's so little of you to love,' she would complain. There were other memories. As a girl, enjoying a tea party with spoons as dolls. 'You're the dream I had for a daughter,' her mother had said. 'You and me in the whole world,' she said another time. 'You're my number one,' she said the day her father announced he would be remarrying. 'Nothing else matters.' Ruth was still a child when her new life arrived to bite her. The three members of her family became two. They moved in with her aunt's family who had a cherry tree in the garden which hid, or tried to hide, the railway tracks. Her mother became full to bursting with feelings but kept them contained in her body so she fizzed as she walked. She once dented the washing machine with a vicious kick. If Ruth cried, she would say, 'I can't help you to help yourself.'

And then there are Grace and Sara. Earlier that week, they sat on the sofa and watched a YouTube video showing an elk taking ages to jump over a fence. Sara and Grace had seen it multiple times, but for Ruth it was new. Separated from the herd, the lone elk trailed the perimeter, back and forth, unsure, trying, judging, running, and finally leaping. 'I feel so sad,' said Ruth afterwards. She said it seemed too much a metaphor for life. 'It takes some folks ages to get to where they want to be, and when they get there, it's a couple of people, or none, who care.' The girls made her drink a cup of tea and suggested an early night.

Ruth doesn't know how long she stays in the cupboard but when the door opens years may have gone by. Crowded into view are the man and his toddler, Rabbi Rebecca and the girls. All are frowning and Grace's face is tear-stained.

'Phantasma?' the rabbi says.

Ruth nods. 'I'm fine,' she says. There are more people

Gemma Seltzer

nearby. A woman wearing a dress printed with a leaf design much like wallpaper. The security guard with her earpiece. Another man, this one with a pointy beard.

I should've made space for this when the girls were small, Ruth thinks. As a child in this synagogue she sat beside her mother who was swollen with anger, while the other children had a father to gaze at through the partition. She hates the memory. But her girls would have had each other, and Ben was around, too. Ruth presses her body against the back of the cupboard.

'All the items,' Rabbi Rebecca says. 'For the food bank?'

'The food bank. Right, Mum?' says Grace.

Ruth's mother was the only person who might understand if she said she was afraid for her children and also afraid of them. Ruth looks at Grace, and at Sara. 'I let you both down.'

'No problem,' says Sara, arms folded.

'What's this lady's name?' asks the white-haired man, speaking to everyone but Ruth.

'For the record, I did my bit. I did what you wanted me to,' says Sara.

Grace elbows her sister. 'It's not important, now!' She turns to the man and says, 'Her name is Ruth.'

'To be honest, half my life I've wanted to hide in a cupboard,' the leaf-dress woman says, sitting down by the cupboard door and arranging the fabric of her dress around her.

'Well, that's nice,' says Ruth, with some suspicion in her voice. 'What kind of cupboard?'

The woman doesn't hesitate: 'Airing cupboard.'

Ruth stretches out her legs and crosses her ankles. 'Warm

there, I suppose,' she says. 'But you couldn't stay for a long time. Too uncomfortable.'

The toddler's grandfather kneels on the floor. 'Ruth? Good Biblical name. I have a nice cupboard under the stairs. I tell my granddaughter it'll lead her to Narnia.'

The man with the beard says, 'I'd choose the cupboard I keep my records in.'

This was getting silly. Ruth says, 'I bet there are heavy doors. It would be hard to breathe.' He shrugs, suggesting they must agree to disagree. He wears a diamond wedding ring, so maybe his record cupboard is spacious and well-ventilated.

'What's her full name? She looks like someone, and I'm trying to work out who,' says the grandfather.

'Excuse me Aaron, while we prioritise what you need over anything else happening right now,' says the leaf-print woman.

'I was just asking.'

'Honkytonk,' says the rabbi.

One by one they sit down, discussing cupboards they have admired. 'In the art room at school,' says Grace, 'there's a cupboard filled with tubes of paint, paper, ink and brushes and stuff. I'd go there.'

'I like that,' says Ruth. 'Plenty to occupy you.'

'Did you ever come to synagogue?' says the man, Aaron. 'You look like one of our old members. She stopped coming, but I remember her. She had the same face as you.'

'No,' says Ruth. She appreciates him trying to find a connection. *These people are strangers,* she thinks. What she wants is to avoid anything happening to any of them. Ruth wonders if the rabbi would say life isn't a set of weighing scales. Or, would she say it is? 'I need to think,' she says, and closes the door again. Nothing happens except everyone else stops talking. Ruth peers through the slats and sees that they all remain sitting, like a puppet show audience. She opens the door.

'Sausages, sausages,' says Rabbi Rebecca.

Aaron is undeterred from his memory trawl. 'I'm trying to recall her name. It's on the tip of my tongue.'

Ruth pulls the door closed and there's silence again, except for a walkie-talkie crackling with a faraway voice. It's calm and the dusty darkness covers her like a blanket. Ruth thinks a great deal about erupting volcanoes creating seismic sea waves.

Later, when she opens the door, a few of them have plates of food. Falafel and challah, pickled gherkins and stuffed olives. 'That looks nice,' she says.

'I think I'm thinking of someone else,' says Aaron. His toddler is gone, and he has a chair, and a newspaper on his lap.

Rabbi Rebecca rushes into view and leans near the door. 'Your bladder must be strong,' she says. 'Or do you need a jug?'

'No, no,' says Ruth, with a little pride. She's always had a robust constitution.

'The weather has turned wild again,' says the leaf-dress woman. 'I don't blame you for staying put.'

The rabbi says, 'It's God. I'm going to call His mum. He's not playing nicely with the other children.'

'She's never done this before,' Sara says to everyone. 'Honestly.'

'We all have our moments,' says the man with the beard.

'But are you okay, Mum?' asks Grace.

Ruth nods and grins, holding up a finger to suggest she just needs a minute. Behind the closed door, she thinks about how mosquito outbreaks will kill families upon families of birds.

The afternoon is spent that way. Talking for a while with these people, then closed within the cupboard to think. Ruth decides there are some things she knows for sure. She has learned basic, intermediate and advanced first aid with St John Ambulance. She can sing in tune. A natural in the garden, she can recognise plants that soothe and plants that poison. She can navigate, she can sail a boat, she can use a hacksaw. Plus, she's not alone, is she?

Parched

It's mid-morning and Ricky is in her bedroom crying during a Zoom meeting. The graduate intern Maria leans towards her computer camera. She has a necklace the shape of a human brain that appears large on-screen.

'Poor Ricky,' says Maria.

Jay glances up from some important phone scrolling. 'What's happened this time?'

Meanwhile, Gordon's mouth is moving.

'You're on mute,' Jay says.

Gordon edges closer to his laptop and surveys the keyboard. Maria's necklace swings briskly in and out of view. It's blue, with etched curves suggesting the brain's surface. They work for a company that designs this kind of bold, colourful statement jewellery. Following a recent restructure, Ricky now heads a team organising online events and this summer they are hosting a festival showcasing women craftmakers with panel discussions and workshops.

'I'm fine,' says Ricky. She wipes a cotton hankie around her nose, watching herself on-screen. Her earrings are laser-cut palm trees. 'I'm more than fine.'

'You don't look fine,' says Jay.

'Shall we get this delivery plan pinned down?' Tears slide silently down Ricky's face.

Jay presses some buttons and soon everyone is gazing towards a colour-coded spreadsheet.

It's mainly Ricky's handiwork, but still she says, 'This is looking good, everyone.' Then, 'Can we check the task durations feel comfortable?'

No one responds. They didn't expect to be living in a virtual world together with their bare faces framed in rectangular boxes on each other's screens, and not all of them are trying to make it work. Instead, Jay complains about their department director. Maria offers a number of new ideas, including a live streamed dance party. Gordon makes a case for leading designer liaison for the festival. He says he'd be happy to spend as much time as necessary supporting the women. In every meeting he mentions this desire.

Ricky's doorbell chimes and she tells her team she'll be back in a moment. A thumbs up emoji pops up on-screen from Maria.

'I'll get it!' Ricky calls to her boyfriend. He works as a games designer and has three computers set up in the living room. She runs into the communal hallway and then downstairs, hooking a cloth mask over her mouth.

'Package for you,' says the delivery man, considering his tablet.

Ricky sobs silently, picking up the box from the doorstep.

The man looks up and his hands drop to his sides. He says, 'I'm so sorry. God, I'm so sorry. Are you okay? Whatever news you've had, whatever's going on—'

'What?' says Ricky. 'Oh this?' she points to her face. People always react so desperately to her when she cries. 'I'm totally fine.'

'Time is a great healer,' the man calls through the gap in the door as it closes.

Ricky returns upstairs to the flat and leaves the box in

the hallway. It's something for her boyfriend. They live in separate worlds during the daytime, meeting for dinner, which they take turns to cook. Recently, their shared experience has felt either tense or hugely entertaining depending on what they watch on Netflix in the evenings.

Back at the desk, her eyes are occupied with tears. Thick ones splash onto the wooden table, and she dips her finger in the puddles. 'Where were we?' she says and listens to the team speak about which deadlines they like and which ones they don't. The doorbell chimes again. She mutes herself on Zoom and shouts, 'I'm on a call!' Her boyfriend sprints down the stairs. 'Firm timescales by tomorrow morning,' she says, closing the meeting.

'If you need to talk…' says Maria, remaining on-screen. 'Are you okay? Monday blues?'

Ricky is glad to tell someone about the park earlier that morning. A young father was teaching his daughter to ride a bike. He jogged alongside her while holding the saddle and handlebars. The little girl wobbled, terrified, with her feet barely reaching the pedals, and the father kept saying with great tenderness, 'I won't let you go. I won't let you go.'

'Beautiful,' says Maria, eyes glassy.

'It was so nice.' Ricky then steps lightly towards the fact of Maria's mother in hospital. It turns out she's had news of a new concern from the doctors.

'But don't worry about me,' says Maria, twirling her necklace. 'You have your own things going on.'

'No, no,' says Ricky, confused. 'I'm fine. I'm only crying.'

Maria says again, 'If you need anything…'

'If *you* need anything…' replies Ricky. What was the matter with people today? Why did they think she was desperate for attention? They were only tears!

After the call, Ricky holds a tissue to her leaking nose. Outside, she can see basil plants, mint and geraniums in window boxes. People kept themselves busy, didn't they? Hand-drawn pictures of rainbows were tacked to windows and on front doors. When the bell goes yet again, she sighs and heads downstairs. Monday morning and so many letters and packages stacked in everyone's cubbyhole.

Ricky unlocks the door, opens it wide, and finds herself staring at three women. They stand motionless on the front path. Each wears a sleeveless summer dress and has long, loose hair. The women all have a face streaked with tears. They look at her for a moment before turning to walk single file uphill. Each moves with orderly steps as if they are following a known route.

Energy zips around Ricky's body while she stands on her doorstep. The streets of Ladywell are quiet except for a couple of vans driving along. She calls her boyfriend, 'I'm heading out for a bit!'

Ricky follows the women along the road, passing a spiky monkey puzzle and the florist's dark shopfront. She loses sight of them but spots what she thinks is the third woman's dress, disappearing between a set of garages. Ricky sees a gate is swung open to show a stairway, part-hidden in shadow. She bounds down the steps. At the bottom, a taste like burned toast hangs in her mouth as she moves through a narrow passageway. Stray brambles scratch her legs.

Soon, the pathway opens up and she is in a garden. Hawthorn trees grow short and stocky with lots of flat, creamy flowers. There are fruit trees dotted around and pink roses growing by the fence. Ricky rubs at her ankles, brushing away the sand. The air is smooth and sweet. At the end of the lawn, almost hidden by a set of wide plane trees, are around fifteen women. The three she saw outside her window stand among them. Eyebrows are animated, and hands gesture above and around bodies. A woman with short, tightly curled hair rests a tub of hand sanitiser on her hip and turns from person to person offering squirts.

Vivid sunlight hits Ricky's shoulders through a break in the leaves. She pauses to lean against a tree, watching. People hold tissues. Some have red eyes. Two older women, both on chairs, let teardrops slide down their faces.

One says, 'No one ever said to me as a child, "Have a good cry." We were hard people.'

The other turns her head. 'Where did you cry?'

'I had a great technique. I was proud of myself. I'd press my face under my pillow at night and cry for a count of ten.'

'I'm so sorry. You must have suffered.'

Ricky isn't prepared for the sudden rush of sensation travelling from her heart to her throat. She walks along the gravel blinking into light that seems stronger as she steps closer.

The woman with the sanitiser raises her hand and meets Ricky's eyes with her own. 'Hello,' she says. 'You're here.'

The next morning, Ricky is up and dressed before dawn. A breeze stirs the bedroom curtains. 'I'm popping out,' she whispers into her boyfriend's ear. He opens his eyes briefly and tells her to take a jumper in case it's cold.

Ricky follows the footpath into Hilly Fields. On the bench

near the basketball courts, she waits. It's hard to know what to expect. She really doesn't know if she can summon tears at will. Ricky always considered her tears as friends calling on her unexpectedly. She's usually pleased, or at least intrigued, to see them. She had a neighbour like that, once. A child who would ring the doorbell continuously too late at night. While her mother looked down and explained it was bedtime, Ricky and her sisters would stand pyjamaed on the stairs staring at the little girl with a skipping rope.

A woman in a patterned headscarf approaches and takes a seat. She rubs her left eye. Ricky nods slightly. These are the signals they have been taught.

'It wasn't always like this,' the woman whispers. 'They used to say thank you when I cooked, now they spit out the food on the plate. One by one. My boys. They think they're men. They enjoy doing it. Spitting like that.'

Sadness washes over Ricky's body. 'I'm so sorry. Sounds incredibly hard.' The sons sounded awful. Children damage their parents with that kind of relentlessness and then they grow up filled with regret, but it's too late to apologise. She looks into the woman's eyes. Ricky feels a flock of tears slip along her own face. 'I'm sure you're doing your absolute best.'

'Oh,' says the woman, her face surrendering to feeling. 'I am. I am.' Her shoulders lift and rise, lift and rise, and then she begins to cry. 'It's just so hard.' She weeps into both her hands.

'I know,' says Ricky. 'I know.'

Approaching New Cross, the roads are busy with delivery

Gemma Seltzer

people, builders and men in suits talking outside buildings. Shops nearby have shutters down. Ricky stands outside the fire station, a grand building with enormous red doors, tall turrets and many windows. A woman walks towards her pushing a wheeled frame and pausing for her feet to catch up. Ricky has a tissue tucked in her sleeve which she now draws out and waves.

When she finally reaches Ricky, she says, 'You came.'

'Of course.'

'I only have ten minutes.' She wears a padded jacket with a floral print and her chin is lifted in that way some people do to suggest defiance.

'Perfect,' says Ricky. 'Tell me how you are.'

'I've named it Derek,' says the woman.

'Derek?' Ricky feels a prickle behind her eyes.

'This feeling I have. I call it Derek. I say, "Hi Derek." "It's you, is it Derek?" "Here again are you, Derek?"'

'Not a welcome visitor, then?'

There is no answer for a while. Traffic lights hold a row of cars in place, before changing and letting the vehicles move forward.

Finally, the woman's face becomes wet with emotion. 'I hate him,' she says. 'I hate him and I wish we'd never met.'

Ricky checks the location on the app. The booking came in as she was on a call, but she was still the first to pick up the request. When she arrives at the launderette, a woman is sat against the wall, legs outstretched, drawing on her cigarette. Ricky nods and pretends to review the ceramic tiles around the shop window. 'Lovely weather,' she says.

The woman throws her cigarette into the gutter. She has

a jay cloth thrown over one shoulder and wears leather slippers. 'Is it?'

'I think so, anyway.'

'I have no opinion,' says the woman. She digs in her pocket for her cigarette packet.

Ricky has been trained for the more challenging clients. There are questions she could ask and her own stories she can offer. Usually, though, Ricky prefers just to stay with the person until they feel ready to talk. So, she sits a few metres away from the woman, knees up to her chest, staring ahead. She's cleared her diary of meetings. The streets are empty. In the distance, a car door slams.

For as long as she can remember, Ricky has cried. She was good at it. She once wept at the top of the Eiffel Tower when her French exchange partner, in limited English, managed to tell her she was boring. It was her highest cry. Another time she cried with her dad on a tourist boat meandering through a disused slate mine in North Wales. Every person on board had a dim helmet torch and they drifted slowly past wax figures posed together to reveal different elements of local history. It was sad to be away from real life, so deep beneath the surface. That particular memory makes her cry and tears charge out and along her face at speed.

'Okay,' says the woman, after a while. 'Okay.'

Ricky turns to see a tear on the woman's face take a winding journey from her lower lashes and along the ridge of her nose. It glides onto her shirt.

'Use the cloth,' she says and encourages the woman to press it to her skin.

Ricky hopes the smell is of washing powder, lemons and calm.

Maria is filling the chat box with comments. She has found an all-female community of watchmakers based in Liverpool and wants everyone to see their work. As she tells them about the collective, she's also searching the internet and sharing bios and links. It's Monday again, and another team meeting. Ricky watches the team scan their screens, clicking and frowning. She's surprised everyone by staying dry-faced throughout.

'Which one are we looking at now?' asks Jay. Behind them, a ginger cat wanders along a tabletop and settles by a heavy brass lamp.

'The red and white watch,' says Gordon.

'No, Gordon! The white with pink,' says Maria. 'For god's sake, I'll just send it again.'

Gordon shifts the conversation to a recent email. Apparently, one designer was not happy with Jay's tone in a recent meeting, so Gordon thinks he should take over managing the relationship. He's pasted extracts from the conversation into the chat box.

Maria is devastated. She wants Gordon's words deleted, as it's disrupted her flow of information. 'Why did you do that?'

Ricky nods but her mind is full of the women she's met over the last few weeks. She thinks about the one with the sons. How was she and did the crying help? The hardest part of the new role is not knowing what happens with the clients afterwards. She's like the delivery people carrying parcels around the country. They may squeeze Jiffy bags, sniff envelopes and speculate about the contents, but they never see the moment a package is opened.

A private message pops up on Ricky's screen from Jay. *Aren't you going to say anything?*

Ricky keeps her face blank as if she hasn't seen Jay's note and smiles into her computer. Let them work this out, she has other things to consider. For example, were tears ever really a problem, or were they a solution? Or were they something else entirely?

'We've been very impressed with you,' says the woman with short, curly hair. Her name is Anita.

'You have?' Ricky can't help smiling. It's been almost two months since she began. The clients submit a score out of five for each meeting, plus an optional review. Ricky's rating is currently 4.9, which places her in the top tier.

'We only work with the best, you understand,' says Anita. 'Those who understand crying at a deeper level. Who have crying as a regular, honed, even daily practice. Those who *are* their tears, who are ready to use those tears. Sound like you? I think it does.'

'Yes,' says Ricky.

Anita had asked to meet Ricky in the garden. It's the home of one of the community leaders, a woman in her seventies who has lived in Ladywell for decades. 'Good,' she says. 'We've had a few hay fever sufferers, in the past. Ditto a few who well up at films, especially when the love interest, inevitably with floppy hair, dies. We consider them amateurs. There is no place for them here.'

Ricky watches a speckled blackbird pick at the flower bed, busy in its search for food.

Gemma Seltzer

'We think you're part of the elite. We believe you're ready.'

'Ready?'

'To tackle the angry women. The ones who snarl. Trickier to manage but we've been waiting for the right person who we think can handle it.' Anita speaks in a firm but slow voice, as if she is a trained athlete swimming an easy breaststroke but could switch to a powerful front crawl at any moment. 'These ones are, shall we say, off the books. Your instructions will come directly from me.'

'I'm not sure,' says Ricky.

Two young girls sail by on scooters. Their faces are covered in delight. Anita says they are the community leader's granddaughters.

'We've been running the Lewisham chapter for years,' says Anita. 'Lockdown has intensified demand all across the UK.'

It's hard for Ricky to digest this information. 'Hold on. There's more of us?'

The girls on scooters are doing loops of the garden and appear again, happy with their speed and the warm wind through their ponytails.

'We have safety precautions,' says Anita, but shrugs as if these are not even worth considering.

Ricky twists the blanket between her fingers. She would like her own scooter and to journey through great spaces of light and air. To go round and round, safe and contained within these surrounding fences.

Anita continues. 'I wouldn't want you to waste your gift. You can support your community in such a meaningful way, especially during these uncertain times.'

Within Ricky, thoughts dart and dive. She wonders, what's the worst that could happen?

The destination for the first meeting is the station platform in Honor Oak Park. The sun is bright and the railway bridge's corrugated white covering glows. Ricky adjusts her face mask and looks to the departure screen. It's five minutes until the next train but no one is waiting. She stands by the vending machine. Eventually, there are footsteps and a woman appears, filling the empty space with her height. Her face, even behind the shawl covering her nose and mouth, is sullen.

'Be careful of me,' she says. Her whole body is storm-charged.

Ricky gestures to the station seating. 'Please,' she says.

The woman carries a stifling, ominous atmosphere. When she sits, somehow a glass drinks bottle is dislodged from the seat and tumbles to the ground. They both watch as it rolls from side to side and eventually stops by the woman's feet.

'Don't worry,' says Ricky.

'Do I look worried?' The woman prods the bottle with her heel.

Ricky wants to say something soothing to disturb the rage visible on the woman's features. Something about bees nearby, maybe? How one just landed on the flowery cone of that buddleia jutting through the railing. 'Bees love blossoms, don't they?'

The woman stiffens. 'Is that the best you can do?'

'Of course not,' says Ricky, although she did think the bee was interesting, the way it lifted itself from plant to

Gemma Seltzer

plant, pausing for every tiny piece of pollen. 'Okay, you tell me. Where shall we begin?'

'Here,' says the woman and she boots the bottle onto the track with force, smashing the glass into pieces.

Should she let herself go now or does the woman need more time? Ricky wonders. Turns out she doesn't have to decide as the tears start to fall. 'Why did you do that?' she asks.

'I don't know,' the woman says, shrugging. 'Just felt like it. Something to do.'

Ricky stares at her carefully and adjusts her face covering. When she was a child, she always felt the potential for something special to happen when she cried. How magical that your body could produce such a pure, clear sign of emotion. A whole language she was born understanding. It was like she could grow feathers. Her tears today are pleading, each one watched by the woman from the corner of her eye. Minutes pass, maybe longer. 'Do you want to continue?' Ricky asks, wiping her nose with the back of her hand. 'I can go and leave you alone?'

'You'd like that wouldn't you!' The woman is on her feet and at the vending machine. She's kicking it and jamming strong fingers onto the keypad. 'Dumb thing,' she yells as she batters her shoulder against the glass, trying to make it shake, but it's firmly attached to the ground. 'None of it was true, none of it!'

Ricky's heart is pounding. In her purse she has some coins she could offer but thinks the snacks inside the machine are not what the woman wants. She raises her voice. 'What's not true?'

'None of what they said was true!'

A child on crutches, one leg plastered to the knee, swings onto the platform. After him comes a young woman carrying overnight bags, a hot water bottle and a large teddy. By the vending machine, Ricky's client calms at the sight or maybe because they have company. Her fists dip into her pockets, bulging there. She sits back down and slumps against the bench.

'Are you okay?' asks Ricky, softly.

'What I'd like to do,' says the woman in a low voice, her nose reddening. 'What I'd really like to do is bury my face in the hollow between someone's neck and their shoulder and scream.'

'Yes,' says Ricky. That's all. She looks at the railway bridge and more buddleia plants on the opposite platform. The woman's clenched teeth relax, and sudden wet tears trickle into the edges of her mouth then beneath her jaw. Ricky keeps her own body motionless, staring ahead. Only the movement of the bees nearby disturbs the stillness.

The next meetings follow a similar pattern. Ricky would arrive nervously and, at some point, would start crying. The client eventually would too. It was tough and involving, but satisfying work. The stories were like waves from a roaring sea, ready to crash down. All she had to do was keep her feet firmly on the ground. Except one day it changes.

She meets a client in the Horniman Museum grounds, and they settle to talk on the trunk of a fallen tree. This woman lives in Forest Hill and describes a childhood scene that has reappeared in her mind after more than thirty years. 'I saw a trailer filled with sheep, bleating noisily. Each had its

Gemma Seltzer

head locked in a brace. The animals were separated neatly into three rows.'

'Feel the rising pressure in your chest and abdomen?' Ricky says to the woman. 'Give in to it.'

'No, no. I can't!' She has more of the memory to share. 'Listen.' The trailer rocked back and forth while the sheep jerked their bodies backwards, their legs in futile race away from their fate. This part of the story is told and retold a number of times. 'One sheep tried particularly hard to shuffle backwards, bending its legs, pulling its body hard.' The woman looks to the sky where an airplane sails behind the distant clouds. 'It knew it was going to die.' The woman repeats this line, and starts from the beginning again. 'I saw a trailer filled with sheep...'

Ricky tries to follow but finds there isn't anything new for her to latch onto. The woman's voice is disconnected from the moment. She's no longer saying words but making a series of strange sounds that slide around like invisible snakes. Ricky realises to her terror that she can hear the words but just can't understand their meaning. She feels hot, choked, and then she feels nothing.

The woman notices. 'I believe you are supposed to cry now?'

Ricky stands up and edges away. 'I'm sorry I can't do this today.' She shakes her head.

The woman calls after her. 'To whom do I speak about a refund?'

Ricky begins to test her tears. She slams her fingers in a cupboard, waiting for the feelings to surge. But nothing.

Joni Mitchell's early albums are beautiful but leave her empty. The same is true of documentaries about genocide and missing children. All the talking heads and archive footage lulls her into a steady stupor, a medley of information she tries to process but can't. For dinner most evenings, she chops mounds of onions. While this shocks her eyes and produces teardrops, it always passes quickly and without emotion.

She arranges a meeting with Anita in the garden. 'I don't cry anymore.'

Anita shrugs. 'Sounds like you've met a blocker,' she says. 'It's not uncommon when you start to cry on demand. Don't worry. I can help. Now, close your eyes and think of something sad.'

Ricky does as she's instructed.

'Right,' says Anita. 'What are you thinking about?'

She's alarmed. 'My head's hazy,' says Ricky. If a gust of wind blew and threw grit from the gutters into her eyes, causing them to itch and stream, she'd be pleased. Anything to prove her tears were still with her and her capacity to feel deeply was not irretrievably lost. That her skin hadn't lost its porousness to take on the emotions of others, absorb them and offer them back into the world for people to see.

'Well,' says Anita, like a parent dealing with a difficult child. 'Picture a dog.'

'What kind?'

'Up to you. What kind of dogs do you like?'

Ricky roams around her head, looking for a dog. She discovers buckets and notebooks. There seems to be plenty of plug sockets. Eventually, she comes across a shiny-eyed Border Collie wandering with its tail wagging. It sniffs excitedly and trots over to an extension lead abandoned on the ground. The dog is clear and distinct then flickers like a faulty light bulb.

'Good girl. Now imagine you are crouching to stroke it.'

Ricky dips down in her mind to pat the dog.

'What's his name?'

'Orpheus.'

'Nice. Now, find a ball and throw it for Orpheus.'

She looks around. There is an old anorak and two silver candlesticks, but no ball. 'I'll have to find one,' Ricky says. She wanders for a while until she locates a box. Thankfully, it is filled with sports equipment. 'Oh good,' she says, 'a tennis ball.'

'Finally,' says Anita. Her voice is accompanied by a rustling sound and crunching. 'Okay, now lob it into the distance, and let Orpheus find it. Enjoy yourself!'

It is fun to play around with Orpheus for a while, and they run through a meadow together with Ricky throwing the ball into the distance and Orpheus dashing back and forth. The sun is lovely, there are buttercups and daisies dotted everywhere.

'Oh no! Oh no!' cries Anita suddenly. 'Watch out Orpheus!'

'What is it?' says Ricky, chasing after the dog in her imagination.

'A speeding troupe of motorbikes,' says Anita. 'It's so noisy!'

Ricky knows she needs to run but finds she is fixed to the spot. 'Orpheus!' The motorbikes are gigantic, with massive wheels ripping into the meadow and marking the soil with their deep treads. 'Out the way, Orpheus!'

Anita pats a rhythm on her legs. 'Orpheus, move! Call him! Oh no! He's coming but oh! He's following your voice! He's heading straight into the path of the motorbikes!'

'Be careful!' calls Ricky.

Anita claps her hands together. 'Bang.'

Ricky sees Orpheus's flattened body under the wheels of a motorbike. She squeezes her eyes shut and calls out his name.

'I'm so sorry,' says Anita.

Ricky opens her eyes. 'Orpheus?'

'He's gone.'

A line of tears forms under both of Ricky's eyes.

'See?' says Anita. 'I believe Orpheus might be a useful tool for you. I use concrete pouring from a great height into every room of my childhood home. Works every time.' Anita's features are set in a smile. She draws out her phone. 'Right, let me check emails to see where we'll send you next.'

Ricky blinks several times. She wrestles with the image of his bloodied body as wet drops hurry down her face. 'I can't…' she begins, but her body remains on the blanket. She used to be friends with her tears. Now she has to kill dogs for them.

Maria is vigorously taking notes. Her new necklace is from the company's new collection: it's a fire extinguisher, carved in wood.

'Everyone okay with the last-minute replacement to the first panel?' asks Jay.

'Sadly, we don't have much choice at this stage,' says Gordon. He feels awful for the designer who pulled out due to illness and asks if he should send her some flowers.

It's a few days before the festival and they're running through the final checklist. Ricky squeezes her cheeks as hard as she can, willing her eyes to flood. She is haunted by the image of Orpheus and the motorbike's huge, rolling wheels. Ricky knows she should speak, she's the boss after all, but her thoughts are hiding under blankets. Every so often one pokes its head out from under the covers, but quickly withdraws again.

Maria's face is big on Ricky's screen. 'It says you have an unstable connection.'

Ricky clicks around for a while, then slams her hand on the table. 'Can't any of you make any decisions without me?' she says to the boxes. They weren't real people anyway, just flat faces with too much junk piled on top of their wardrobes. She abandons the meeting.

In the evening, Ricky's boyfriend shows her how to work the controls for a new game he's created. It's called *Furlough* and the aim is to gather sparkling coins which equate to days paid without work. People in suits appear from office building doorways, but you can shoot them down and continue to fly around gathering money.

'This is fun,' says Ricky as her character points the pistol at a figure holding a clipboard.

That night she lies awake running through the event programme for the festival and trying not to think about Orpheus. In the early hours when the light is pale and bluish, she rearranges her pillow and curls around her boyfriend's warm body, before finally falling asleep.

Ricky is early for Maria's one-to-one on Zoom. As she waits, she stares at the chest of drawers reflected on-screen. Perhaps she should put a plant on top. Ricky looks to the side at her wall map and sips from a glass of water. Earlier, she marked the locations of her clients. The London Borough of Lewisham told through the bodies of weeping women. In Blackheath and Greenwich, they cried understated tears, not wishing to bother anyone. When Ricky thinks of Brockley, it's bloodshot eyes and many words to describe an emotion some people would simply call fury. Places like Lee and Deptford had women who held in feelings for so many years.

'Hello!' calls Maria from the laptop.

Ricky tilts her screen so Maria can see better. 'Look at this,' she says. 'All the places I've cried this year.'

Maria leans closer as Ricky points out a few of the locations, not mentioning the other women, only that she'd covered a lot of ground recently. She pauses as she describes crying outside the launderette and the scent of washing powder. The boy on crutches and the bee are included, too. Ricky adjusts her laptop angle. Her face feels dry and abandoned. She decides she might call her dad after all these years.

'Well, hopefully it's out of your system now,' says Maria, who wears gold earrings in the shape of wings. She wants to jump straight in, she says. She asks for permission to share thoughts on the upcoming Instagram takeovers.

'Go ahead,' says Ricky. While she listens, she thinks that if crying *is* out of her system, what's left inside? Just arid, barren space and emptiness. Where's the good in that? She always had so many tears, she could afford to give them away!

Gemma Seltzer

Maria speaks about a designer who makes necklaces with bullet-shaped capsules to store tampons.

'Very nice,' says Ricky. Maybe she needs to refill the well before beginning again? She holds up her glass to the screen, feeling wild and crooked. 'Hey, look at this!' she says and pours the contents over her head. The jolt of water floods and flattens her hair, sliding down her forehead and neck.

Maria breaks into spontaneous laughter, as if she's never laughed in her life before. 'Ricky! What did you do! Crazy woman!'

Water from Ricky's soaked shirt drips steadily onto the carpet. She laughs too and it comes from deep inside her. Soon it gets caught in her throat, she begins coughing and then laughing some more. Maria laughs too and tears stream down her cheeks. For the remaining forty minutes of their meeting, they sit together in their separate homes, on laptops connected to the same server, and look at each other laughing and crying. Lush, lovely tears. Bleak, uncertain tears. Elated tears. Sad tears. All kinds of wonderful tears.

Acknowledgements

All the stories in this collection were drafted while walking in London, and are influenced by the experience of navigating the city on foot. They weave in overheard conversations, memories and inspiration from articles and books read at the time. This includes work by individuals I look to with wonder and admiration: Lydia Davis, Amelia Earhart, Lauren Elkin, Bernardine Evaristo, Amy Hempel, Sheila Heti, Edna O'Brien, Frank O'Hara, Yoko Ono, Grace Paley, Sylvia Plath, Robert Frost, Jean Rhys, Rebecca Solnit and Virginia Woolf.

Huge thanks to Gary Budden, Sanya Semakula and the team at Influx Press for the perceptive feedback and excellent advice, which guided the collection into its final form.

This is a book filled with the voices of women, and I'm delighted that the cover typeface we chose for the collection is Lelo, by talented designer Katharina Köhler, discovered on Typequality.

Thank you to Rachel King and Cherie Nelson at Ruminate magazine for publishing 'Should a Catastrophe Occur' and to Sylvie Bertrand and Christopher X. Shade at Cagibi journal for publishing an earlier version of 'Other Esther.'

I'm grateful to many people and organisations for supporting my writing journey, including Sarah Butler, Maura Dooley, Tania Hershman and Ross Raisin, the

Arvon Foundation, the Literary Consultancy and the London Library.

Without the honesty and wisdom of Emily Haworth-Booth, Sophie Herxheimer, Sarah Malin, Shazea Quraishi, Anna Stearman and Alison Winch, this book would not be in the world today. I can't thank these brilliant, generous women enough. Hooray for Claire Berliner, Emily Bromfield and Katrina Naomi, too. Thank you for your writerly friendship.

Thank you to my grandpa Sammy Seltzer, the first ventriloquist I ever knew, to puppeteer Bronia Evers and to the UK Ventriloquist Club for advice and inspiration.

Thanks to the amazing Write & Shine community for rising early in the morning and joining me on the creative path.

I'd love to thank the following people for their support and conversation, and for wandering around London and other cities with me over the years: Charlotte Aston, Annette Brook, Laura Cattell, Wing-Sie Chan, David Cross, Kristin Dasgupta, Lily Rose Davies, Wallis Eates, Georgina Fox, Louise Hillyer, Mark Hopkinson, Miriam Lessar, Helli Mason, Stephen Nash, Emily Oliver, Franklyn Rodgers, Silvi Shrestha, James Trevelyan, Célia Vermicelli and Emma Whiting. You are tremendous.

I dedicate this book to my incredible friends Rachel Cherry, Cecilia Magill and Amy Racs. I always hoped I'd find such deep, long-term friendships and I'm so glad to have you in my life. To my family, especially my parents Gerry and Lynne Seltzer and my sister Carly Seltzer, for their encouragement, their stories and a lot of laughter. And, most of all, to Mathew Hanratty for unwavering support, so much kindness and so much joy.

About the Author

Photo by Lauren Renner

Gemma Seltzer is a London-based writer. Her work includes the *Guardian*'s award-winning virtual reality film 'Songbird,' fictional blog '5am London' and online flash fiction series 'Speak to Strangers,' subsequently published by Penned in the Margins. She collaborates with dancers, photographers and older adults to create writing and storytelling projects. Gemma has written for BBC Radio 3, performed her work at the Venice Biennale and runs Write & Shine, a programme of early morning writing workshops and online courses. gemmaseltzer.com

INFLUX
PRESS

Influx Press is an independent publisher based in London, committed to publishing innovative and challenging literature from across the UK and beyond.

Lifetime supporters: Bob West and Barbara Richards

www.influxpress.com
@Influxpress